TEXAS

HAWKS MC NEXT GENERATION

USA **TODAY** BESTSELLING AUTHOR

LILA ROSE

CHAPTER ONE

MAYA

"*B*aby—"

"If you call me that again, I'm going to punch you in the balls, Texas." I glared down at the injured man lying on the bed in a guest room at the Hawks MC compound. He'd not long gotten placed there, the room clearing of club members for me to work after an altercation down the street. Currently, he wasn't feeling the pain I knew he was in, thanks to the strong medication I'd given him. Still, it didn't mean I had to listen to him, or this new pet name—instead of little Marcus—while I worked.

Earlier, when I'd been called to the scene after Texas had been jumped by a bunch of wannabe thugs, and before he got saved by a woman and her two dogs, I'd thought it would be an easy fix on the scene.

It wasn't.

While I hadn't been told all the details of what had happened—and I probably wouldn't get *all* the information—what I did know was that the situation would be taken care of privately through the Hawks motorcycle club. This is even though Texas wasn't yet a member, but he was a friend of the club, and his uncle was the president to the Caroline Springs Charter in Melbourne. Actually, we'd both been brought up around the club. My dad was the main boss over all the Hawks charters around Australia, but we resided in Ballarat.

Having grown up in the club meant I wasn't surprised when someone got hurt from "certain situations." Only now I could do something to help. I'd been called in because I'd become their own personal doctor since I completed my Bachelor of Paramedic Science degree. Although, it was lucky I'd been available, since usually I worked odd hours and a lot of them.

Texas's irritating smirk brought me from my thoughts. He was probably thinking I secretly enjoyed his new pet name. Did he still think I had a crush on him? Annoyance and embarrassment burned under my skin. I hated the reminder of my crush and how I used to look at him with puppy-dog eyes. In fact, it made me want to press a little harder on his cracked ribs, which was what I did, drawing out a pained wheeze from him.

"You done that on purpose," he accused, scowling.

"Yep." I nodded. "So don't be a jackass and call me endearing names." I checked over his other side and found two more cracked ribs. "Besides, my boyfriend wouldn't like it."

"The prez know about that?" he clipped.

That would be a hard no. A very hard hell no. Dad was as protective of me as a dog was to its bone. Actually, growing up surrounded by a bunch of men in an MC made my dating life pretty much nonexistent. Except, this time, I was lying my arse off. I didn't have a boyfriend, but Texas didn't need to know that. I lied because whenever I was around Texas, he either flustered me or annoyed me. I wished he'd just forget the crush I had on him or the fact my brother had pretty much begged Texas to teach me to kiss because I'd been scared of messing up when the time came.

Nope, I couldn't, wouldn't think about that moment or how he'd said, "Not bad, little Marcus." He'd ruffled my hair. "I'm sure someone will like it."

Pushing that night from my mind, I sighed. "No, Dad doesn't know, and you won't say anything." If Talon knew, there was no doubt my imaginary boyfriend would have a background check and drive-bys from the MC brothers in seconds, and if I gave the name of some poor fool, their lives would change instantly.

Texas hummed under his breath.

"Texas, I mean it. Do not say a word."

His frown was replaced with a cocky smile. "What do I get in return?"

I wanted to kick him.

Why was he this flirty version of himself with me now? He used to dodge me every chance he got because I was only his friend's little sister.

Ignoring his question, I placed myself in doctor mode and treated him like I would any other patient. "Sit up. I'll wrap your ribs and clean your cuts and scrapes, but then I have to get going."

With my help, Texas sat. I could feel his gaze on me, but I didn't meet it. I worked on his body. On his hard, tattooed body.

Ignore it.

Ignore those hard plains, those dips and bumps of his muscles. I pushed his looks aside and worked so I could get out of there. The sooner I wasn't around him, the better. I hadn't been honest with myself before. To me, my feelings back in the day weren't just a crush. When I'd been a teen, I'd *loved* stupid Texas Monroe.

What I thought was love anyway.

Now that I was older, I was smarter.

At least, I liked to think I was, and realised it had been a young, foolish crush. The only reason Texas still got to me and my emotions was that over the years he'd grown from an attractive boy into a man who you wanted to make a body pillow out of. What helped was that he knew what he wanted in life and went for it. He'd just opened his second tattoo business in Ballarat, while his first was in Melbourne. He had skills. People from all over the country sought him out for his art to be tattooed on their bodies.

He was smart, funny, cocky... and I had to learn to forget about him. He'd made it obvious I wasn't his type with the women I'd seen him dating. They were everything I wasn't. I was sure he went out of his way to date all women who had a different hair colour than my dark brown. They were all tall, slim, sweet, shy... unlike me. I got my strong will from my mother and attitude from my father.

Sighing, I went about packing my things into the bag and stepped back from the bed. "It'll take six weeks to heal those ribs. Please take it easy or you'll make them worse." Turning, I started for the door.

"Maya," Texas called softly.

My heart liked it. My heart wanted me to face him, smile at him, and take care of him.

My heart was a fool and needed a punch.

"Yes?" I stared at the door.

"Thank you."

I paused for a moment. "Okay" was all I said instead of "You're welcome." I may have been acting petty, but I needed the distance between us for my heart's sake because it was willing to cling to anything he gave me.

Opening the door, I stepped out and closed it after me, forcing a smile for the man in front of me. "Hey, Dad."

"Kiddo," he replied, opening his arms to me. I

wrapped mine around his waist as he curled his around my shoulders. "How'd it go in there?"

"Good. He has four cracked ribs, several cuts, bruises, scrapes, but no concussion. Still, it's probably best to keep an eye on him."

Our hands dropped away, and I smiled up at him. Dad bopped my nose. "And how're you doin'?" He was always worried about his kids. Even though I wasn't his biological child, he'd claimed me. Which was good, because I'd claimed him right back. He was the best dad anyone could ask for. Though, he could tone down his protectiveness. His brows dipped. "You look stressed. Those fuckers workin' you too hard?"

Rolling my eyes, I shook my head. "I'm fine. How are you feeling?"

He placed the back of his hand to my forehead. "Don't stress about me, but are you sure *you're* okay?"

I lightly slapped his hand away. "Stop worrying. Now, I've taped his ribs and cleaned his wounds. He'll probably sleep for a while, since the meds have kicked in."

He curled his arm around my shoulders and steered me down the hall. "Thanks for comin'."

As I was about to answer, we heard, "Wanna say thanks also, Maya." Dodge tipped his chin up to me as he walked our way. We stopped and he placed a kiss on my cheek. "The club would be lost without you." He ruffled my hair like I was still ten years old and not twenty-one like I actually was.

"You know I'd do anything for you guys, even when you annoy me."

Dodge and my dad, Talon, chuckled. "Gonna go see him. Catch up soon," he told Dad.

"Got it." He nodded.

Before Dodge left, he added, "Maya, come on down to Melbourne. Low will wanna spoil you for a while."

"Someday soon." I smiled. But there was no chance I'd visit, since Texas lived there.

Dodge winked and left to go into Texas's room as Dad's phone chimed with a message. He pulled it free, and his brows pinched as he read whatever it was.

When his jaw clenched, I knew he wasn't pleased. Slowly, he pulled his gaze back up to me and I swallowed thickly. "What?"

He crossed his arms over his chest and stared me down. "Somethin' you wanna tell your dear old dad?"

Scrunching my nose up in confusion, I shook my head. "No. Nothing."

Dad lifted his phone and tapped it against his chin. "You sure?"

Since I hadn't done anything bad recently, and the last time he yelled at me was when I took Swan to an adult store when she was underage and the sales assistant tried to sell us cocaine, I couldn't think of anything that would upset him.

"I'm sure."

"Then you wanna tell me who you're datin'?"

Anger gripped my belly. That arsehat mofo couldn't

even wait until the next day to inform my dad I was dating someone. Who did that dick think he was?

Sighing, suddenly more drained than before, I shook my head. "Let me guess, was that Texas messaging you?"

His jaw clenched again. "If it was?"

"I only told him I was dating someone because... well, he was annoying me."

"Did he ask you out?"

"Dad, no. He's not into me—"

"Are you into him? I remember back in the day you were. Are you still holdin' a candle for the guy?"

"No. I'm not for him or anyone. Besides, work takes up all of my time at the moment." He didn't look convinced. "Seriously, there's nothing and never will be anything between Texas and me. You have nothing to worry about." I gripped his arm and gave it a squeeze. "I really should go, though. I need to get some sleep before my next shift."

He studied me for a beat longer and then nodded. "I'll see you at home."

Home.

Some days, I still couldn't believe I lived with my parents, but then I knew moving out would be more of a hassle than I needed right now. Only the need to get out soon was growing. I wanted to see what it would be like to have a life without my parents breathing down my neck. Not that I didn't love them for caring. Sometimes it was a little overbearing.

"Yeah, I'll see you there." Reaching up, I placed my

hand on his shoulder and kissed his cheek before I made my way out of the compound. Once outside, that anger from before twisted inside of me again. Taking out my phone, I pulled up my contacts and was about to press in Texas's number to shoot off an aggressive text but stopped.

It wouldn't be worth it.

There was also a chance that if I gave Texas more of my time, even with texting, my feelings for the man could sprout and grow once again. I couldn't let that happen. Years ago, I'd beaten them to a pulp and shoved them way down into the pit of my stomach. They weren't to surface again.

I was older now, somewhat wiser, and I knew Texas wasn't for me.

So no, I wouldn't text him and spiral down that hole again.

There was someone out there for me. I just had to find him.

After I'd found my own place where I could bring someone home without having my dad standing over whoever it was, ready to rip out his throat if he said or did something wrong.

Yes, it would be best to wait.

Unless someone caught my attention beforehand. Someone I could laugh with. Someone I could trust and know they were genuinely interested in me.

By the time I got home, Mum was standing in the kitchen in her dressing gown, sipping a cup of coffee.

She smiled warmly. "You were out early."

"Had to help Dad with something." I moved over to give her a hug.

She cupped my cheek when I pulled back. "You look tired, sweetie."

A yawn overtook me, and she laughed. Nodding, I grabbed a granola bar. "I am. I'm going to head to bed. Get a nap in before my evening shift. Leave a note if you're not around when I wake and let me know if you need me to do anything."

Mum shook her head. "You already do enough. Drake and Ruby could do more around here. Which reminds me, I need to wake them up for school. Have a good sleep, sweetie."

"Thanks, Mum. I'll see you tomorrow."

Her lips thinned, but she forced a tight smile and nodded. Mum hated the long and different hours I did, but it came with the job. A job I enjoyed because I could help people in need. Not all of the calls had good endings, but so far, I'd managed to learn to deal with the bad situations. Though, from what I'd been told from my colleagues, apparently what I'd seen to date was mild compared to some of the nightmare ones.

Finishing the granola bar, I walked into my bedroom and threw the wrapper on the top of my dresser drawers. I grabbed some clean pyjamas and went into the bathroom, which thankfully was adjoined to my room or else I'd have to fight Drake and Ruby for usage time.

Turning on the shower, I stripped out of my clothes

and adjusted the water before stepping under the spray. As soon as I closed my eyes, my mind took me to Texas. The image of when I'd seen him on the couch with blood coating him was stuck in my head, causing my heart to drop, like it did at the house.

The thought of Texas hurt gripped my stomach violently once more. Only I wasn't supposed to care. I wasn't supposed to worry if I'd left him too soon.

Sighing, I shook my head, picked up the shampoo, and pushed thoughts of him from my mind.

CHAPTER TWO

THREE MONTHS LATER

MAYA

"*J*'m surprised you're here with how much you've been working."

I turned at Josie's words and smiled. In the next second, we were hugging. Officially, Josie was my aunt. She'd been adopted by my grandparents when I was young, but now she was more than an aunt. As I grew older, she became a best friend.

"Question is, what are you doing here?" I asked. Josie had moved to Melbourne when I was about eight and now lived happily with her two husbands and twins.

She shrugged. "Missed everyone. I was also sick of

FaceTiming and calls when I wanted to really *see* how Talon was going."

My stomach tightened and a wave of sadness swept over me. Dad had been shot a month ago by Cody's girlfriend's father. He took a bullet to save Cody, and we'd nearly lost him. It was a time I never wanted to relive again. Mum had been a mess and had only started to leave his side longer than just getting my brother and sister to and from school.

My throat clogging with emotions, I cleared it. "I've been keeping an eye on him. He's getting there." I gave her a watery smile. "Though, he thinks he's ready to be up and running like normal. I give him another month before Mum lets him get back to work."

Josie reached out and squeezed my hand. "It's lucky he sees how wrecked Zara was and is allowing all the mothering."

Nodding, I shifted to the side to let Killer and Ivy slip by before I nodded towards the back door. I needed sunshine to warm me. To help fight away the cold of the memory of Dad getting hurt. As we made our way out, I said, "That's true. God only knows he could do with the rest, though. Anyway, where are your husbands?"

She laughed, stepping outside into the sunny afternoon. "Probably following the twins around to make sure they don't get into too much trouble."

Laughing with her, I spotted Swan, Rommy, and Clary approaching, and smiled. We ended up talking about things we'd been up to lately, and I was about to ask

Rommy something when I happened to glance to the side and stilled when I saw Texas standing near the back door with my brother Cody, Ruin, and Wolf, who was Ruin's partner.

He was talking, yet his gaze was on me.

Only I didn't understand *that* look. I'd never seen *that* look in his eyes before. I wouldn't even know how to describe it. Soft, yet something else.

Whatever it was, it sent my stomach a flutter, so I quickly glanced away and swallowed.

"Are you okay?" Swan asked softly. She always spoke quietly.

"Yeah, yes. I'm fine." An awkward laugh followed. "Just spaced for a second."

"You won't believe what I saw the other day," Rommy said. Our friend was always full of stories and fun. She wore her heart on her sleeve, and everyone couldn't help but want to protect her.

"What's that?" Clary asked.

She leaned in. "Porn."

My eyes widened, and mine weren't the only ones.

Rommy shrugged. "It was surprising. I've seen books with naked ladies in them from when Texas hid his under his mattress. But what I don't get, and wanted to know, was do women really like their hair being pulled? Or like having a guy's shlong shoved down their throat?" Her head tilted to the side. "I mean, she acted like she liked it, but her eyes watered a lot and there was so much snot. Is that something you lot like?"

Swan turned beet red. She hadn't done anything with anyone and probably hadn't even watched porn. At least I'd had one experience. Even though it was in the back of a car and awkward as hell.

"Um...," Clary mumbled, glancing around wildly.

"Well...," Josie started. "I guess, ah, maybe sometimes."

Rommy hummed under her breath and nodded.

"Rommy, what you see in porn isn't like real life, usually. A person can like a little hair pulling and such, but just remember porn stars get paid for what they do, which is act."

Clary pointed at me. "Yes, they're actors. When the time comes, you'll find things you like and dislike. Just be sure you're honest with your partner."

Rommy smiled. "Okay." She saw something that caught her attention. "Oooh, brownies." Then she was gone, skipping off to get her treat.

"She's such a sweet soul," Josie said.

I snorted. "Sweet soul who asks about porn. I never thought I'd hear that come out of her mouth."

Josie, Clary, and I looked at one another and started laughing. Swan's blush spread down to her neck, and she covered her warm cheeks with her hands.

My laugh tapered off when I could feel eyes on me. I chanced a glance over and saw Texas looking. I glared. The arsehole grinned.

Texas was freaking me out. He happened to turn up at places where I was. I hadn't thought he was in Ballarat still, but there he was. In the last few weeks, I'd seen him show up at a café, the supermarket, and the compound. Okay, so that one could easily happen. But what was weirder was how he'd try and start a conversation with me. Which shot nerves right to my belly. Every time I'd quickly make something up and run the other way.

I couldn't handle his warm smiles. They caused my blood to pump through my body too fast, making me near dizzy.

He'd never paid attention to me before.

Then why now?

Was it to mess with me?

Shaking my head, I walked into Cody's Harley store and smiled at Cowboy. "Cody in?" I pointed up at where Cody's apartment was above the store.

He nodded but then shrugged. "I was sure I saw Coyote not long ago, but his woman was with him."

Well, dang it.

"I can walk in first."

I spun at the voice, my smile settling into a scowl at Texas who stood just behind me.

He grinned. "So you don't have to wash your pretty

eyes out in case you see your brother in a position you don't want to."

I snorted, crossing my arms over my chest. "Yeah, I'm sure you'd love to see Channa in a— You know what, never mind." With heat in my cheeks, I faced Cowboy. I couldn't believe I'd burst out with that. It didn't matter that I thought Texas had been flirting with Channa the night he'd got injured. It wasn't like she saw anyone else now she was with my brother. He was her world. That was plain to see. "Tell my brother to call me."

Cowboy looked from me to Texas and back again before he nodded slowly.

I went to pass Texas, but he grabbed my upper arm. "Why wait? Scared to be around me, *Maya?*"

How dare he say my name in that low, rough tone.

If I could grip my heart and shake some sense into it, I would.

It was hard to admit my little crush was still there. Down deep. *Way* down deep. It was why I didn't want to be around him more than necessary. Far too easily, I could let it spark again.

Knowing what kind of man Texas was made it possible for feelings to get attached.

Other than the fact he was a flirt, he was success-driven and kind. He'd help out anyone if he could. He was careful and sweet to not only his sister, but Dodge and Low, his guardians.

Still, I was and would always be just his friend's sister. Someone he'd known from a young age. Someone who used to follow him around. Someone who had her brother make him kiss me.

He wouldn't see me as anything more.

But then why was he popping up everywhere?

Why was he flirting with me with those smiles?

Gah, shut up, mind.

Tipping my chin up, I glared at him. "Scared? No."

Mirth filled his gaze. "Good." He used my arm to turn me. "Then you'll come up with me."

"Wait, I didn't...." He kept dragging me. "I have to be somewhere."

He glanced over his shoulder, his gaze reeling me in. "It can wait."

"It can't. I have to..." What? *Think of something, dammit.* "Clean my car before I go to bed and start my shift."

"Uh-huh." He stopped at the bottom of the stairs that led up to Cody's place and faced me, dropping my arm. "How is work?"

How is work? Why was he asking?

"Good." I nodded. "How's the ribs?" His cuts and bruises had all healed, at least.

He patted his left side. "All better. I had a good doctor." I rolled my eyes. "How's the boyfriend?"

"Boyfriend?" I blurted, and then it dawned on me. I'd told him I was seeing someone. "Oh, ah, he's good." I thumbed over my shoulder. "Anyway, I better go." I took a step back.

"He's good?"

"Yep." I nodded.

"I noticed he wasn't at the hospital when shit went down with the prez."

Why had he noted that?

"He'd been out of town. He travels a lot." I took another step back.

Texas cocked a brow. "Really?"

"Yes. Anyway, tell—"

"Maya," Cody called from the top of the staircase.

Shit. I'd nearly made my escape.

Cody led Channa down with his hand in hers. He noticed Texas standing there. "Hey, brother." He'd always called Texas brother, even when Texas wasn't a member of the club. They had a close bond, one they also shared with Ruin.

"Hey," Texas replied and turned a grin on Channa. "Darlin'."

The taste on my tongue soured. I ignored it.

"Texas." Channa smiled. "Hi, Maya."

"Hey, girl." I'd come to care for Channa a lot. She was perfect for my brother, and it was good to see him as happy as Mum was with Dad.

"Maya was too scared to come up in case you two were gettin' it on," Texas teased.

I shoved him and shouted, "I was not."

Channa blushed, while the other two idiots chuckled.

As I scratched the side of my cheek with my middle finger, I grumbled under my breath that I was going to kill Texas.

What nailed his coffin shut was when he reached out and ruffled my hair.

Like I was still his friend's sister.

Like I was still a kid.

I brushed his hand away. "Cody—" I pointed at him. "—I'll call you later. Channa—" I smiled at her. "—I'll be at the bakery later in the week." Looking at Texas, I pulled my upper lip high. "Asshole, see you never."

"Maya—"

My hand shot up in his face. *Up* because the dick was tall. "Nope." I quickly rushed out of there with a tightness in my chest.

Get it through your head, Maya. He will only ever see you as a kid.

CHAPTER THREE

TWO MONTHS LATER

MAYA

*W*eariness tugged at my mind and body after I woke to my alarm. It was going to be one of those rough days when my head already thumped with a headache. Groaning, I sat up in bed and twisted to place my feet on the floor.

Of course, the first thing that swept through my mind was how I hadn't seen Texas in a couple of days. Yet before that, it had been the same. He'd somehow managed to be around wherever I was and tried for a conversation. Every time, I made excuses and bolted.

Sighing, I scrubbed a hand over my face. I really had to

stop dodging him. It wasn't his fault a part of me had clung to him and wanted more.

That damn first kiss had sealed the deal with my heart.

Well, it would just have to get over it because in a few days I was going on another date with Samuel. He happened to be one of Drake's teachers who I'd met one time at school when I had the chance to pick up my brother and sister. We'd clicked that day, and our words had quickly turned flirty. I'd enjoyed our first two dates. He made me smile and laugh. He was easy to talk to.

The sexual energy would grow.

It would.

It had to.

The date coming up would be our third, and I planned to go further than kissing and fondling to see if the small connection we'd been building over texts, calls, and a couple of dates could ignite into something more than surface interest.

Samuel was a nice guy.

He also didn't run when Dad opened the front door half naked and pointed at his wound, stating, "I got shot saving my son. Imagine the lengths I'd go to keep my daughter protected."

Samuel had looked a little scared, especially when Dad then pulled a hunting knife from the back pocket of his pants and waved Samuel in.

Thankfully, I'd come running from the hallway and ushered him back outside. I could see he regretted coming to the door, especially when I'd originally told him I'd meet him at the car. I'd thought that would be the last date, but by the end of the second one, he'd asked me out again.

I was looking forward to it.

I was.

Sort of.

I thought I was.

God, I didn't know.

I liked Samuel. I just wasn't sure if I saw something more than friendship with him. Maybe it would be best to cancel over text. No, that'd be rude. I'd meet with him and tell him I was messed up in the head and heart.

Standing from the bed, I made my way into the bathroom and took a refreshing shower that helped my headache a little. Once dressed in my work uniform, I snuck out of my room so I wouldn't wake anyone and went down into the kitchen. Since it was nearing midnight, it was still dark outside. I turned on the light above the stove to brighten the room enough to see. I pulled the refrigerator door open to grab something I could snack on until I bought a big breakfast somewhere on our break. But when I saw a packed lunch with my name on it, I smiled. Mum must have noticed I stopped making my own lunches when time got away from me, especially since I preferred to get an extra ten minutes of sleep than be prepared for the day. It made me sound lazy, but my body was revolting at my messed-up sleep patterns.

After driving in a daze, which wasn't good, I dragged my feet into the depot.

"Maya."

I turned towards the doorway off to my left when I heard a familiar voice. Smiling, I made my way over to Easton.

"What are you doing here?" I asked as we hugged.

"They're low-staffed and called in a couple of us Melton people. How have you been? Are you getting used to the hours?"

I shot my brows high. "Do you ever really get used to the hours?"

Easton laughed and shook his head. "No."

"How's Parker and Lan going?"

It was cute how his face lit up at the same time that he blushed. "They're good. We'll be at the next family barbeque at the compound, since we missed the last one."

"Great. You don't want Mum and her posse coming after you three."

He chuckled, shaking his head. "No, we really don't."

"Maya, come on," John called from our vehicle with a wave.

Reaching out, I pressed a hand to Easton's elbow. "I'll see you soon."

"You will, and we can talk more about work."

Nodding, I gave him a grateful smile. "I'd like that."

By the time John and I were on the road, I knew it was going to be a quiet night. There hadn't been a call in over an hour. It was great for everyone else, but the quiet only made things harder for me to stay awake.

"Favourite food?" John asked as he drove.

I laughed. "Haven't you already asked me that?"

"Have I? Shit, I can't remember."

"It's the old age getting to you."

His glare only made me laugh louder. "Shut it, girlie."

Reaching out, I patted his arm. "It's all right, John. Aging happens to everyone."

"You make me sound like I'm on my last legs. I'm not, smartarse."

"Well, this smartarse could really go for a nice hot coffee to keep her awake."

John snorted. "See how awake this old man is, girlie? I could run rings around your tired form."

Rolling my eyes, I couldn't help but smile. I loved working with John. He reminded me of a mixture of Dad's club brothers. He also never minded if I gave him hell with the teasing. We'd gotten along from the first day, and I couldn't have hoped for a better partner.

When he pulled into a twenty-four-hour petrol station where we knew the coffee didn't taste like arse, I smiled over at him.

As he stopped the vehicle, I undid my seat belt. "You want the usual?"

"You know it." He took out the romance novel that he'd been reading for a while and opened it. His wife, Moreen, loved to read, and he decided to check out some of her choices. He hadn't been a fan of the polyamorous romances but didn't mind romantic comedies. I thought it was cute how he read them so they'd have something to talk about.

I'd just grabbed the coffees and John's donut when my phone rang. I glanced outside and saw John waving wildly.

We'd gotten a call. Finally.

I quickly threw the cash onto the counter and ran outside. John took the coffees and placed them in the holders while I got strapped in. We took off with the sirens blaring.

"What's the call?"

"A bystander at a party said a guy collapsed. He's breathing but not responding."

"How far out?" I asked, taking a sip of my coffee.

"Ten."

I'd managed to get my coffee down by the time we stopped in front of a house that looked like it could use a makeover. There was music pumping from inside and lights flashing. A group of people stood in the front yard.

John and I grabbed our bags and made our way up the path. My partner opened the gate and called out, "Paramedics. We got a call about someone unconscious?"

"Yeah, over here." A guy pointed down at the ground on the other side of a huge tree, and then he took a sip of whatever was in his cup. Once around the tree, I realised the people outside were all gathered around a prone form on the grass, staring and talking. "He's probably just drunk," the same guy said.

"Step back," John ordered. They all did, just not far.

"Move back more, please," I tried. They took another step and watched us work like we were a new television show.

John tapped on the unconscious guy's cheek, and surprisingly, he opened his eyes. He smiled. "Oh, hey," he called and tried to sit up.

We pushed at his shoulders to keep him in place.

"Please don't move until we look you over. Do you know why you're on the ground?" John asked.

The guy laughed. "Yeah."

I flicked the penlight over his eyes. Glassy, bloodshot, and wide pupils. Could be alcohol or drugs or a mixture of both. I glanced at John, and he nodded in understanding. "What's your name?"

"Phil." He looked up at me. "Man, I just need something.... I'll be fine."

"I don't think that's a good idea, Phil. You've had a few drinks, right?"

He chuckled. "A few, yeah."

"Maya, he has a cut on his leg that looks infected."

I nodded. "Phil, how long have you had a sore leg?"

He waved a hand around. "Don't feel it. It's not sore." He pushed at my hands. "Going home. Just tired."

"Phil, how about you take a trip with us first? You can have a sleep in the vehicle while we take a look at your leg?"

"Nah." He went to sit up and groaned, lying back down. "Feel dizzy."

"Okay, Phil, just relax. John will go get the gurney, and we'll wait here."

"You sure?" John asked as he glanced around at the other people.

So far, the onlookers had stayed back, chatting and laughing among themselves. I couldn't see them being a problem. "Yes." Besides, I knew John wouldn't be long.

I patted Phil's shoulder. "Just rest there for a moment." Glancing at the others, I asked, "Does anyone know Phil?" While I listened to the answers, I checked over Phil's vitals.

"Never seen him before."

"Nope."

"Didn't he come with Brad?"

"I don't think so. He showed up with Gail."

It seemed no one knew Phil. Why was he at a party where no one knew him? It didn't make sense unless someone inside knew him. Right then, I guessed it didn't matter. We had a patient to treat, and that was what we'd do.

John came back, and together we got Phil onto the gurney and into the back of the ambulance.

Phil groaned and gripped his stomach. "It hurts."

I stopped checking over things and pressed down on his stomach. Phil moaned when I touched his right side. When John got into the driver seat, I called out, "John, maybe appendicitis."

"All right. We're heading to the right place to get that fixed."

Phil groaned again as John started to drive.

"Phil, are you hurting anywhere else?"

"Head... just, just give me something to take the pain away."

I was already reaching for the pain relief when I paused. "Let me check your stomach once again. Appendix is on the left, so tell me if it hurts." I pressed on his left and he groaned. Phil was lying. Thinning my lips, I caught John's gaze in the mirror.

"Give me something," Phil ordered. "Anything. Just make it go away."

"How much have you had to drink?" I asked.

"Doesn't matter. Give me drugs." He glared up at me.

Just as I looked at the restraints, Phil reacted. He punched the side of my head, and I instantly saw stars. The vehicle swerved, and I heard John cry out.

"Pull over, pull over," Phil ordered.

I blinked repeatedly and wondered why John was moaning. When my focus cleared, I saw Phil raise a knife and stab it down into John.

"No!" I cried and lunged for Phil. He turned and kicked out, but I managed to get my arms around his waist and take him to the floor.

"—under attack. Help," I heard John say and prayed the call went through.

A sharp pain to my lower back had me sucking in a breath and my grip on Phil loosening. My head was jerked backwards by my hair, and he pressed the knife under my throat.

His stale breath washed over my face when he said, "Get me all the drugs you have in here."

"O-Okay," I whispered. Panic clutched at my heart. My body shook, my pulse feeling like it wanted to leap from my skin. *Calm down and think, Maya, think.* "J-Just let me check on John and—" I whimpered as he slid the sharp edge down the side of my face.

"Now, bitch. I want it all now." He shoved me back and pointed his knife down at me. "Move."

Nodding, I got to my knees and went to the locked drawers. I grabbed a garbage bag to lay on the floor between my knees. My hands shook and I fumbled with the keys as I tried to unlock the first one. I needed to go slow. John called for help. They'd be here soon. Right?

John.

A sob caught in my throat as tears welled.

Please be all right. Please.

I cried out when I was suddenly knocked forward from a hit to the back. "Hurry up, bitch."

My head throbbed, but I managed a nod, biting my bottom lip to try and control myself. I couldn't lose it. I couldn't break. John needed me. I had to help him.

"M-Maya," I heard from John. He sounded weak, tired.

"I-I'm okay," I called. I didn't want him to worry, to try and help me. "I'm all right." I heard him shifting up front and then he groaned. "John, please, you just stay there." I grabbed whatever my hands landed on and dumped them into the bag. Drugs weren't worth getting us killed over. I had to get Phil out of here as soon as—

Sirens sounded in the distance. I froze for a second and glanced at Phil.

"Fuck," he spat. "They heard his call. Fuck." He turned John's way.

"No," I cried. When Phil faced me again, I held the bag out. "Take it and go. *Please.*"

His jaw clenched. "Open the doors and get out."

Get out?

He wanted me to get out with him?

But I needed to see to John. It didn't matter that my head and body throbbed. I needed to help John, and I couldn't do that if I got out with him. What would he do to me if I did? Would he let me go?

I shook my head, tears welling. "Please, take it and go so I can help John. Please, Phil."

His jaw clenched over and over. The sirens grew louder. He thrust the knife my way and nodded to the doors. "Open the fucking doors and get out."

I had no choice.

I had to do it.

I couldn't look away from the knife. If I could get it away from him, the situation could turn in our favour.

Did I dare?

Was it the right choice?

When Phil kicked out at me, I lunged for his knife-wielding hand and grabbed his wrist. He held on and gripped my hair, trying to pry me off him. My hair felt like it was torn from my head when I leaned in and bit him.

His hand opened and the knife dropped. I managed to kick it under the bed before his hand wrapped around my throat and he threw me into the doors.

My mouth opened and closed, trying to draw in a breath. My eyes watered as I gasped, coughed, and eventually sucked in the air.

But Phil was there. Right in front of me again. The doors opened behind me. I tumbled out onto the ground with a cry and groaned.

Sirens sounded close. Engines revved. Tyres screeched. People shouted.

I was picked up and held against a chest. A sharp needle point stabbed against my neck.

Help had arrived, but was it too late?

CHAPTER FOUR

TEXAS

*M*aya was always on my damn mind. Always close to the surface when I saw something that reminded me of her. It'd been like this for a while now. Ever since I saw her at a family barbeque, standing in a ray of sunshine and talking with her friends. When she'd thrown her head back and laughed, my damn breath had caught. Then when she smiled, I'd pretended it was just for me.

That day, that moment, had been like a bomb going off in my chest. Like my heart had woken up with a zap. Though, even before that, I'd admit that for the last few months, my heart had been ticking just for Maya and her attention.

She'd always been a stunning girl, but now she was a

LILA ROSE

gorgeous and smart woman. Someone I wished I'd taken care of instead of how I'd brushed off her teenage crush like it was nothing. I hadn't been smart back then.

So yeah, I'd fucked up when it came to Maya Marcus.

Fucked up when I'd agreed to be her first kiss.

I'd been in Ballarat visiting the compound with my uncle and Low. Cody, a good mate and son to the big honcho, had pulled me aside and told me his sister had confessed to him that she'd never been kissed but wanted to learn before she started dating so she didn't look like a fool. He'd told me to kiss her. I did and thought nothing of it.

I didn't know she'd got feelings.

I didn't know I'd hurt her every time I'd rocked up to an event with a new girlfriend under my arm.

I didn't know until her feelings had morphed into annoyance towards me.

There was a chance my ignorance was a good thing, though. At the time, she'd been young. Too young. Shit, at the time, I'd been in my prime teen years, flirting and fucking any girl who paid me attention. I thought with my dick a lot of that time. I hadn't seen just how much I'd screwed up until my goddamn mind, body, and soul was shocked alive by Maya.

Since then, I'd tried to get her to see me as I was now. I made sure I found her at family gatherings to talk, and every damn time, she made an excuse and slipped away. Nothing worked, not even when I'd winked, smiled, or tried to joke with her.

34

She was over me and my ways.

I had to change that. The need to do so pressed on me more recently, ever since I got a wake-up call and knew that no one could predict what could happen on any day. When Talon had been shot and nearly killed, it put things into perspective.

It was time for the next step in life.

Since I'd gotten my businesses underway and thriving, it was time to get the woman.

When I had Maya, and I fucking prayed I would, she'd see she was my world.

Which was why I was back in Ballarat. Besides organising things at my newer tattoo shop and home, I was there to show Maya I'd changed. But along with that plan, I'd also gone to Talon, wanting to patch into the club. It'd been the last thing I wanted to do before I went to Maya and tried to get her to understand she was mine.

I knew that if she'd accepted me in time, after I courted the hell out of her, I'd be the luckiest man in the world.

She was my other half. She just didn't know it yet.

Talon leaned back in his chair and eyed me. "Dodge know you're here, wantin' to patch into the Ballarat charter?"

"Not yet," I told him with a half smirk.

"Why here, Texas? Why not back with your family?"

Maya was here, and she'd want to stay close to her family. Not that Talon knew I wanted his daughter as my old lady. He'd probably kick my arse, but I'd take the beating if it meant I could have the woman.

"I like Ballarat."

His brow quirked. "You like Ballarat?"

"Yep."

"What about your store in Caroline Springs? What about your family?"

"Got a manager I trust for it, and I'll go check on it every now and then. But I'm already set up to run the one here. Got the house attached to the shop as my own also. My family will understand and support me."

"Even Low?"

I couldn't help but huff. "Even Low. Won't deny she'll throw a fit, but she'll do it while helpin' me pack. Besides, it ain't that far away." An hour tops.

He ran a hand over his head. "Maybe you should talk to Dodge first."

"Prez, I'm old enough to make my own decisions." Besides, he already knew.

"Fuck. I know. The lot of you have grown up too quickly."

I snorted. "Scared you're gettin' old?"

His glare snapped my laugh off. "I can still take you down, *kid*."

I believed it too.

He sighed and nodded. Hope shot into my veins. "Fine. I should make you a prospect, but I know Hawks is in your blood, always has been. Give me a week, and I'll set up the ceremony—"

The door opened abruptly. Talon stood up, gun in hand and pointed that way. Where he got the gun from, I didn't fucking know. He lowered it when we saw Killer breathing like he'd run a marathon. Before Talon could say anything, Killer did. "Catch." He threw a phone at Talon, who snatched it out of the air and placed it against his ear.

"Talon," he clipped. "Easton, slow down and breathe. My phone is on silent while I'm in a meetin'.... What are you sayin'?" He stilled, gripping the phone. "Where is it? *Where*?" he barked. "Right," he bit off, then hung up, throwing the phone back to Killer. "Get the brothers who are here. We're ridin' out."

Killer nodded and disappeared. Talon tucked his gun into the back of his jeans.

I stood. "What's goin' on?"

He started for the door. "You're not Hawks yet—"

"Bullshit," I snarled and followed him. "I can help. Just tell me what's goin' on."

He glanced over at me as we picked up into a jog, and I saw it then, the fucking terror in his gaze. His jaw clenched and unclenched. "Easton said there was a dispatch call that got cut off from Maya's vehicle. Someone's taken control of it."

I stopped.

My body.

My heart.

My breath.

Everything except her name running over and over in my head.

Fear had taken hold.

"Texas" was yelled harshly, and I blinked slowly at Talon. He studied me for a beat. "You comin' or do I need to get someone to lock you down?"

"I—" Clearing my throat, I caught up. "I'm comin'."

No one was going to stop me.

Even though my body had kicked back into gear, my mind remained locked tight with pure panic for Maya. Still, I'd managed to work on autopilot. I went to my bike, got on it, and rode off, following behind Talon, Griz, and Blue, because I knew they'd lead me to where Maya was.

Our rides rumbled along as we pulled onto a street where I could easily see an ambulance down the road with its back doors open. Cops and other paramedics surrounded the vehicle, and the officers had their guns drawn. We stopped. Some took notice of us, and even more so when Talon pushed his way through.

"Put it down and let her go," a cop yelled towards the ambulance.

As Talon stopped and cursed low, my gaze snagged on what was in front of us.

My gut clenched.

Blood pumped harder through my veins.

Maya had blood on her everywhere. It dripped down the side of her face. Her right eye was already swollen and bruised.

Near the back of the opened doors to the ambulance,

a guy held Maya in his arms with a needle to her neck. A parked car blocked their left side, and there was enough room to their right for another car to pass by before it hit the curb, a path, and houses.

"Step back," another cop ordered Talon.

Talon didn't. He took another step closer. "You know who you have there?" he called out clearly.

"Just stay back," the guy holding Maya screamed and shifted slightly, taking Maya with him so her body covered his more.

Maya's brown eyes teared when she stared back at her father.

I wanted to run to her, fucking protect her, take her away from this nightmare.

But I couldn't do shit.

I couldn't help because I wouldn't risk her.

Not when he was so close to her. I knew this. The brothers and cops did too.

Fuck.

"This was supposed to work," the guy yelled. "You all ruined this."

"Phillip Newton, you don't want to do this." A new officer stepped forward. "It is Phillip, right?"

"H-How do you know?"

"We went to the same school." The cop took another step.

"Stay there," Phillip yelled. His hand tightened around Maya's arm, and I saw her wince. "I'll do it. I'll inject her." The needle shook where he held it against her neck, just below her ear.

What the fuck was in it?

Inside the ambulance, someone groaned.

"Let them help John," Maya said, licking her dry lips. "I'll go with you. We can run, but let them help John."

"Like fuck," Talon roared.

Phillip flinched.

"Cool it," Griz clipped low, grabbing Talon's arm.

Talon shook off his hold. "You're holdin' my daughter hostage." Some cops cursed around us. "She belongs to the Hawks MC. You do anythin'—"

"Shut up," Phillip screamed.

Maya cringed, but she kept herself together. Kept still, like she was calm, but I saw the frantic look in her eyes. "*Please*, Phil, just let them help John."

Fuck me, of course she'd worry about someone else and not herself.

Movement off to the right side caught Phillip's attention just as I spotted cops trying to sneak that way. He dragged Maya this way and that. "Stop or I'll do it. I'll kill her. I will."

Everyone froze.

"Back up," Phillip yelled. "I want the street cleared behind us and a car full of petrol."

"Phillip, we can't—"

"You want her to die?" he snarled, shaking Maya by her arm.

Maya bit her bottom lip, new tears welling.

It fucking broke my damn heart to see.

I unclenched my jaw. "We gotta do somethin'."

Anything to get him away from her.

"All right, Phillip. Calm down, and we'll get things sorted," the cop who knew him said, his hands out, pressing down on the air. He turned and muttered a few words, and another cop took off at a run.

"Dad, tell Mum I love her," Maya called.

My throat thickened and pressure slammed down on my chest.

Phillip glanced around and around, watching, waiting.

I caught Talon swallowing thickly. Emotions clogged his voice when he tightly replied, "Maya, darlin', tell her when you see her."

She smiled softly, sadly. "Okay. I love you too, Dad."

His bottom lip trembled, and I had to bite down on my own when her gaze flickered to me and back to her father.

Phillip laughed humourlessly behind her. "You're not going to do want I want." He nodded to himself.

"Phillip, we are. It just takes time."

Phillip snorted.

I didn't like the look in his eyes.

I didn't like the way he'd suddenly stopped shaking.

Like he'd accepted something.

"Maya," I uttered.

In seconds, everything went to hell.

Talon bellowed Maya's name and started running. We

followed just as Phillip pushed the needle in and injected our Maya, *my* Maya, with something. Phillip let go of her, smiling as she dropped to her hands and knees. Maya's wide, fearful gaze lifted to us as she gasped. Her hand lifted to grip at her chest before she rolled to her side.

"No" was roared.

It was either Talon or me or all of us.

Shots were fired, and a running Phillip fell, but all I could do was stare at Maya, her hand stretching out to us before she'd slumped to the ground and her eyes closed.

CHAPTER FIVE

TEXAS

*H*er heart stopped.
She died.

He'd killed her, and now he was dead, and I couldn't make him pay.

She just wanted to help people.

She wanted to heal.

He'd made her body shut down.

He took her breath. Her pulse. Her light.

In those moments, I'd wanted to go with her.

In those moments, my heart had cracked before it shattered.

I'd felt it hard, so hard it took me to my knees as I gripped my head and choked on a cry that rent the night air.

People shouted. So much commotion. So much noise.

She was so still. So quiet.

I couldn't look at her. We'd failed.

We'd lost her.

Someone dragged me to my feet, moving me back, wrapping an arm tightly around my shoulders.

"They got her breathin', brother. They got her breathin'." The person shook me. "Get on your ride. We're followin' the ambulance to the hospital."

Numbly, I nodded.

They got her breathing, but would it stay that way?

I ground my teeth together for letting that fucking thought enter my mind.

She *would* be okay.

She *had* to be okay.

Somehow, I managed to make it to the hospital. Yet, as I stood outside the building, I couldn't bring myself to enter.

The ache in my chest wouldn't give in.

The stabbing pain in my gut wouldn't rest.

And my goddamn eyes kept getting wet so I had to roughly wipe at them.

Groaning to myself, I shifted to the side and pulled out my phone. Dodge would want to know. Had someone called him?

"Texas."

I turned at Griz's voice.

"You comin' in?"

Clearing my throat, I nodded and waved my phone at him. "Just callin' Dodge."

He tipped his chin up at me. I didn't like the way he was appraising me. "See you in there."

Nodding again, he went to go through the doors, until I called, "Griz."

He turned back.

"Do you know how Zara is?"

Maya's family had been through so fucking much.

Griz looked grim. "Julian's rounded up her posse. They're bringin' her in."

Jaw clenched, I nodded once more. She had her women with her. That'd be good enough until she could have her man.

"Texas—"

"See you in there," I said quickly and turned my back on him. I didn't know what he was going to say, but I couldn't risk finding out right then because if it was anything deep, I'd crack. I pushed the call button on Dodge's number and lifted it to my ear, facing away from the doors.

"Kid, it's four in the fuckin' mornin'. You drunk again?"

"Dodge—" I clamped my lips together when just his name got caught in my throat.

I heard rustling on the other end and then he said, "Talk to me, Texas. You all right?"

I hummed under my breath.

"Where are you?"

I scrubbed at my face and cleared my throat. "Ballarat."

There was a pause, and then he asked softly, "Is Maya all right?"

Clenching my teeth, I closed my eyes and shook my head. He knew what I'd planned. He knew I wanted Maya as mine, if she'd take me... if....

She'd stopped breathing.

She could have been gone from me.

They got her back... but did it stay that way?

I was too fucking scared to find out.

"Dodge," I managed to get out and then groaned in frustration.

Fucking hell, I couldn't even manage a damn conversation.

I was a fucking pussy.

A jolt shot through me when a hand clamped down on the back of my neck. I lifted my gaze and found Griz there with his hand out. Dropping my head, I handed the phone over to him and closed my eyes, clenching my jaw.

"Dodge, it's Griz. There was a situation where Maya's ambulance got taken over. The guy... fuck, he injected her with somethin'. She stopped breathin' for a while. They got her back before they headed to the hospital. We're here now, headin' in to see how things are." He paused for a beat. "Yeah, I'll let him know.... I've got him, don't stress.... See you soon."

She'd stopped breathing. Her heart stopped beating.

She'd been lifeless.

"Texas."

I opened my eyes to take my phone back and pocket it. "He comin'?"

"Yeah, brother. He's on his way." He shook me a little with his hand still on my neck. "She'll be good."

Clearing my throat, I nodded. "Yeah, 'course she will." *Please make that right.*

His hand fell away. "We headin' in?"

My body locked. A pain in my chest formed.

Tyres squealed behind us, and we turned to see Julian's vehicle skid to a stop out front. The doors opened, and Zara, Maya's mum, was there along with Deanna, Ivy, and Malinda. Julian raced around the hood to get to Zara's side as she lifted her gaze and it landed on us.

Her bottom lip trembled, but she bit down on it. Her feet ate up the concrete, and I thought she'd head straight inside.

Instead, Zara was coming our way, and her eyes were locked on me. "What are you doing out here?"

I drew in a breath through my nose and fucking prayed I didn't show too much emotion in front of her.

"We're headin' in now. Just called Dodge to let him know," Griz answered.

Zara shook her head. "Texas, you should be in there."

Why?

What for?

She wouldn't want to see me.

I fucked that up.

47

But if I had the chance, I'd do anything to win her over. To show her I wasn't the man she'd seen with other women on too many occasions.

Show her I'd finally woken up to see what was right in front of me.

But she didn't need me right now.

"Babycakes, how about we go in?" Julian curled his arm around her shoulders.

She glanced at him and nodded before she looked back at me. "Talon called me. Said the doctors told him she was going to be all right."

The pain in my chest lessened as my eyes widened.

Still, I couldn't bring myself to say anything because the relief was like a rush to my head, and I feared what I'd say.

Yet it didn't matter because Zara watched my reaction.

She gave me a watery smile as tears formed. "She'll need help to recover from this."

I nodded.

"You'll help, right?"

Another dip of my head.

Zara reached up and patted my cheek. "Good." With that, she turned and made her way in with her posse following.

Griz hooked his hand around the back of Deanna's head and kissed her quickly. "Be in soon, darlin'."

With a small, soft smile, she nodded and followed Zara in.

Griz shifted closer to me and elbowed me in the ribs. "You ready?"

With a sigh, I scrubbed a hand down my face. "Yeah." Slowly, I followed him into the waiting room, which was nearly full with members of the Hawks and their family.

Cody, also known as Coyote in the club and Maya's brother, stepped in front of me. The bastard took one look at me and tugged me into a hug. "You steppin' up?"

I unglued my teeth and whispered, "Yes."

He pulled back and patted my shoulder. "'Bout time, brother." Channa, Coyote's woman, moved close with a soft smile, and Coyote hooked his arm around her neck, curling her into him. He tipped his chin up at me. "She's gonna be all right. Mum and Dad are in there with her now."

I nodded. Griz squeezed my shoulder and walked off to his woman's side, who sat with Ruby and Drake, Maya's younger siblings, and Nancy, their grandmother.

Even when we'd lived in different areas, Coyote and I had always been close. I didn't realise he'd seen what I was feeling for his sister. I didn't think, in the last half a year, that I'd shown my hand too much. Obviously, I had, and hearing him accept where I wanted my future to go with his sister meant a hell of a lot.

I just had to win Maya over. Show her she was more to me than anyone else. Show her she wasn't just Coyote's sister.... She was more. She was someone I wanted to spend a long fucking time with.

Coyote glanced over my shoulder. "Fuck."

"What?" I clipped and turned to the doors.

"Mr Nareen." Drake jumped up from his seat and ran over to the guy standing just inside the doors. Drake waved his hands around as he talked to the guy, who nodded. He then smiled sadly and ruffled Drake's hair, but Drake pushed his hand away.

"Who's he?" I asked.

Coyote sighed long and loud before he said, "Someone."

Turning back to him, I crossed my arms over my chest. "Coyote?"

He winced. "Dad told me Maya went on a couple of dates with one of Drake's teachers. Drake must have told him what happened."

Maya had been going on dates.

My blood boiled, but I curled my hands into fists to control the rage. My reaction was more over the surprise of Maya dating, but I had no right to react.

She hadn't been mine.

She didn't know.

Was I too fucking late?

Was she really into this guy?

A teacher?

Christ, why was my chest hurting again?

I was a fucking fool for not noticing what was right in front of me earlier. A fucking fool for giving Maya her first kiss and ignoring that damn spark that shot to my groin over it.

But back then, she'd been too young, and I'd been too stupid and thought with my dick too much.

Now I'd lost my chance.

She was with someone.

How many dates had they been on?

Were they serious?

Had they kissed?

Had he touched her?

"Brother, how about we step outside for some fresh air?" Coyote asked.

"No."

"Um, Texas." I felt Channa move closer, but I didn't look away from that guy. "You're going to burn a hole in the guy's head with that glare, and people are noticing."

Drawing in a deep breath, I nodded and walked back outside. The sun was rising in the distance. It was going to be a nice day, and yet, all I could feel was cold inside.

Fucking fool.

I'd left it too late, wanting my businesses set up and running before I could throw all my attention onto Maya.

Christ. I'd made the wrong decision and only had myself to blame.

"It ain't anythin' serious," Coyote said when he stopped beside me.

"Okay."

"Texas, it was only a couple of dates. He shouldn't even be here. He ain't family. Maya and him aren't tight."

It sounded like he left off the "yet" at the end of that.

"It doesn't matter right now," I told him. "All I care about is that Maya is all right. That she'll get through this night and eventually put it behind her to be happy." Glancing up at the sky, I held back the tears threatening to fall. "That's all that matters." It was. Nothing that I felt in that moment mattered. It all seemed insignificant when Maya was in a hospital bed after dealing with this nightmare.

Coyote's hand landed on my shoulder. "All right, brother. All right."

"Your family's been through so fuckin' much." How did they deal?

"We have, but we have so many people at our backs, holding us up. If it wasn't for the support from everyone, we might not be as strong as we are."

I snorted. "Bullshit. The prez would carry you all." He was a fucking good man. Like Dodge, my uncle who took Rommy and me in.

Coyote chuckled softly. "Yeah, you're probably right."

We stood outside for a while longer and talked when we felt like it. Though, it must have been longer than I thought, because just after Channa walked out to get Coyote for his turn to see Maya, someone called my name.

To the left, I saw Ruin and Wolf walking my way. Ruin had his hand resting against Wolf's back.

"Fuck, brother." Ruin pulled me into a tight hug. He was another close friend who knew about my growing feelings for Maya, other than Dodge and Coyote guessing it. He pulled back and placed a hand against my neck. "You good?"

Clenching my jaw, I nodded. Ruin tipped his chin up in understanding. He knew from one glance that I didn't want to talk about it or I'd crack.

I glanced at his man, a reality which was still mind-blowing. I never thought I'd see Ruin in a relationship, let alone with a guy; he'd never shown interest in men. But fuck, anyone could see they were smitten with each other. I got to see it more when I'd visited them at their place in Melbourne. "Wolf, thanks for travelling with Ruin. We all know he ain't safe on the roads."

Ruin snorted and mock punched me in the gut. "Prick."

Wolf smiled, pushing his blond locks from his eyes. "I'm glad I'm not the only one questioning his skills."

I grinned. "All skills or just with a vehicle?"

"That's it. I ain't standin' here listenin' to his shit." Ruin started towards the doors with his hand in Wolf's. He turned back. "You comin' in?"

"Soon." I wouldn't fuck this up for Maya. If I saw that guy in there, and he went into Maya's room, I didn't know what I'd do.

Maya would always come first.

"See you soon," Ruin called over his shoulder, and I grunted in return.

It wasn't much later when a car stopped in the emergency area. The doors flew open, and Low and Dodge were there.

Fuck.

I ground my teeth together and looked at the ground, blinking rapidly.

"Tex" came from Dodge before he cupped the back of my neck, and my forehead hit his shoulder.

"Honey," Low's soft voice sounded from my side.

"Fuckin' shit night, kid, but it can only get better from here."

A horrid noise sounded in the back of my throat. I wasn't sure. I still felt hollow, cold, and annoyed with myself for worrying about my own feelings when Maya had just been put through hell.

"What the fuck are you starin' at?" Low suddenly snapped. "Yeah, keep movin."

"Little bird, how about we keep from scarin' the people to a minimum."

"What? It was one person, and I didn't like the way she looked at us."

Straightening, I brought her into my chest, chuckling softly. "Thanks, Low."

"I've got you, honey."

"I know." They were my family. They were there when I needed, like I would be for them.

CHAPTER SIX

MAYA

"*D*o you want me to get your parents?" the nurse asked after the doctor left. I hadn't been awake long and still felt off, sore, light-headed, and nauseous, but I nodded. I wanted my family around me.

They told me I'd died.

My heart had stopped beating after what he'd given me.

Blinking slowly, I glanced off to the wall. My brain felt sluggish, like my head was filled with cotton wool.

What happened to John? I hadn't asked.

Why hadn't I asked?

It should have been the first thing on my mind. Instead, I'd just felt relief that I was okay.

Guilt ate at my stomach.

Before I could call someone to find out, the door opened. Mum and Dad were there. Tears pricked my eyes. Mum was already crying as she rushed over and gently hugged me. Through my watery gaze, I met Dad's soft one. Even his eyes held moisture. I reached out, and he took my hand instantly.

"You're okay. You'll get through this. We're here. Lean on us, sweetie," Mum cooed, brushing my hair from my eyes. Her eyes lingered on the cut on my face that was covered by a bandage, the bruises, the swollen eye.

But I was alive.

Nodding, I tried for a smile, but it wobbled. "I know, Mum." When I noticed the nurse who brought them in starting to leave, I called out, "Excuse me." As soon as the nurse looked back, I continued, "John. The man in the ambulance. Is he all right?"

When the nurse didn't answer right away and I looked at my parents, I knew.

My throat closed over as a sob caught. "No," I whispered, my bottom lip trembling. "No."

"Sweetie." Mum tried pulling me close, but I shook my head and pushed her back.

"It should have been *me*!" I screamed. "He has a wife, a family. It should have been me."

He didn't deserve to die.

God. Moreen would be devastated. It wasn't fair. It wasn't fucking fair.

Tears welled and fell, and I pushed Mum back again. A sound I'd never made before broke out of me.

"Sir, you can't—"

"Get the fuck out," I heard Dad bark, and next, I was lifted and on Dad's lap. I tried to get away. I tried to fight his hold. "Darlin', come here. Come on, baby."

"No, no, no." I pushed, I grabbed, I ripped, but Dad just held on to me.

"Baby girl." He locked me in tight and rocked me. "Breathe, sweetheart, breathe."

"Dad," I cried.

"I know. I know it hurts."

"His wife. His family."

"I know. Fuckin' unfair, sweetheart."

I gripped his tee and held tight, crying into his chest. "It should have been me. He had a family."

"No, sweetheart. I won't fuckin' hear it. What happened to him was a goddamn tragedy, but your life isn't any less than his. We...." He cleared his throat. "We nearly lost you, Maya. We know his family's pain. We get it. We can help them. Be there for them. But never say it should have been you, because you're important to many as well."

"Sweetie," I heard Mum say softly and felt her at my back, careful of the stab wound that I knew would hurt worse if I wasn't on pain medication. Then again, they'd told me it wasn't that deep.

But none of that mattered.

The sorrow and guilt were drowning me. I couldn't

stop crying. I couldn't stop picturing John, his smiling face, his laugh, and then how he would have taken his last breath in that vehicle.

Because of that fucking man. I wouldn't say his name. I wouldn't think it. He was nothing.

"T-The man who did this...."

"He's dead," Dad said.

It wasn't enough for me. He should have been alive and suffering. He took a good man from his family. From me.

"I know, kid. I wish he was fuckin' alive too," Dad said without me saying a word. "An easy death wasn't enough for him. He deserved worse."

I nodded into his chest. Was I supposed to feel bad for thinking such things? I didn't know. I didn't care. That man did deserve to suffer through more pain, more heartache. Knowing he wouldn't gutted me.

It wasn't fair.

He got off easy.

"Kitten, shift back. Gonna lay her back down," Dad said to Mum. I gripped his tee tighter. "Sweetheart, your nightie is damp. You mighta pulled some stitches."

I wished I felt the pain. It could numb my head, numb my thoughts. Dad slowly lowered me, and my back tugged, causing me to wince.

Mum pressed the call button as I wiped my face and took a shaky breath. Only new tears welled when I thought of John.

Dad brushed my hair from my face and kissed my forehead. "You'll get through this."

I nodded slightly, sniffing and wiping at my eyes. Mum took my free hand in hers and squeezed just as the door opened and a different nurse entered.

"Can you please check her stitches?" Mum asked.

"Of course." With help from Dad, I leaned forward, my head spinning a little, and the nurse checked them. "They look good, but there has been some bleeding from the gauze moving. I'll get a new waterproof one."

"Thank you." Mum smiled. She looked exhausted. They both did.

When the nurse left, I said, "You two need to rest."

"Maya—"

"Dad, I-I know I lost if for a bit, but I'll be okay." I waved a hand towards the door. "Ruby and Drake are probably out there. They'll need you."

Mum shook her head. "Don't you worry about anyone else but yourself."

But I did. I would, and really, I wanted to be alone. I didn't want to stress them more than I had. We'd all been through enough. "I need some sleep too," I tried.

Mum's lips thinned as she shook her head. "I know, and look, they're only planning on keeping you in tonight, in case of concussion. Sweetie, I'd like to stay with you, please."

Mum had probably already guessed my plan to push them away so I wasn't a bother and could wallow on my own, but she wanted to support me. She wanted to help me, and deep down, I knew I would need and love some type of comfort.

Glancing at Dad, I caught his small nod with a soft smile.

"Okay, Mum. Thank you."

She waved me off. "Don't thank me. I will always be here for all of our children."

"I know."

Dad's hand rested down on my arm. "You up for some visitors?" He felt it when I tensed, and quickly added, "You don't have to have anyone in here if you don't want."

"It's not that I don't appreciate their support."

Dad nodded. "I get it."

"So..." I licked my dry lips. "Would it be okay if I just saw my brothers and sister?"

"Fuck yes." He leaned down and gently kissed my temple where I'd been sliced. "Be back."

When Dad left, Mum pulled over a chair to sit beside the bed. She took my hand in both of hers. "It's a bit crowded out there, so it'll be good your dad sends everyone off."

I gave her a tight-lipped smile and nodded. Weariness suddenly took over. Shifting my gaze up to the ceiling, I had to blink rapidly as more tears formed at the thought of John.

All I could think was how unfair it was to lose such an amazing man.

"You'll be okay, sweetie." Mum ran her fingers over my hand.

"I-I don't know if I could go back to... I wouldn't be able to"

"Hey, work is not something you need to worry about right now. Let's just take each day as it comes. No one will force you to do anything you don't want to do."

Roughly, I wiped at my eyes and drew in a shaky breath as I nodded.

The door opened, and in flew Ruby and Drake. Mum pushed back in time for Ruby to take her place while Drake stood on my other side. Ruby's bottom lip trembled. She leaned in, and I reached out to cup the side of her face. Her tears fell as my eyes filled once more. Ruby bent further and placed her forehead against my shoulder. I put my hand around the back of her head and held her close.

"I'm all right," I whispered, choked.

"Fuck," Drake clipped, and when I looked at him, he spun his back to me. I didn't miss his hands clenching and unclenching at his sides. Dad stepped up to him and gripped his shoulder.

"Drake, come here," I said softly.

"Give me a sec." His tone was tight.

"Drake."

He turned my way, and I caught a glimpse of anger in his gaze before he leaned in and clasped his hands around my upper arm to then push his face into my shoulder. "Fuck."

61

Dad cleared his throat. "Cody will be in soon."

Nodding, I kissed the top of Drake's head and then Ruby's. "Guys, I'm okay."

Drake sniffed and straightened. "If that guy was still alive, I'd fuckin' kill him myself."

"Drake, language," Mum tried from where she leaned against Dad, though it wasn't her usual peeved or annoyed tone when Drake slipped up and swore.

"You'd have to get in line, kid." My gaze swung to the door where Cody stood. His jaw clenched, nostrils flared, and the anger I saw in Drake's eyes burned brighter in my other brother's.

With a weak smile, I said, "I'm okay."

Cody's jaw tightened again. "Bullshit," he clipped. "But you *will* get there."

My bottom lip trembled. "I will." Hopefully.

"Kids, let's hit the road," Dad stated.

Ruby whispered in my ear, "I'm sorry this happened, but I'm here, always. If you need anything, just ask."

I kissed her forehead. "Thanks, sis."

Drake cleared his throat. "Not sure if I messed up, but I panicked and let Mr Nareen know you were here."

"Drake," I breathed as anxiety gripped my chest.

"I'm sorry," he muttered, glancing away from me.

"Hey," I said, gaining his attention back, and when I held my hand out, he took it. I gave him a squeeze. "It's okay. Dad will tell him I'll talk to him soon. I'm just not ready for it now."

"Okay." With a quick kiss to my cheek, Drake walked out of the room, and Ruby quickly followed her twin.

Dad gave me a hug and kiss. "See you soon, kid."

"You got it."

"Kitten, walk me out," Dad said.

"I'll stay while you're gone, Mum," Cody said. Dad laid a hand on his shoulder before leaving.

"Be back soon," Mum said with a wave before she too was gone.

Cody stepped further into the room and closed the door.

"Where's Channa?" I asked.

"In the waitin' room."

"She could have come in," I told him with a frown.

"Said that to her. She didn't want to intrude on family time."

I snorted, enjoying talking about anything else rather than what happened. "She's already a part of the family."

He smirked, taking Mum's chair and pulling it close again. "Said that too, but you know her."

"I do. She's too nice."

His face softened. "She is."

"You picked well for once."

He mock glared. "I always have good taste." I rolled my eyes and stilled when he shifted in the seat and leaned forward. "So, you didn't want to see that teach of yours."

Relaxing a little since he wasn't going to talk about that... and John, I sighed and ran a hand over the top of my head. It was getting harder to keep my eyes open from tiredness. "No. I... I just wasn't ready."

"Texas is out there."

I looked away. "That's nice. Mum said there was a lot of people, or it was Dad who told me... I don't know."

"Maya—"

"Don't. Please."

"Okay," he whispered. "Ruin's also out there with his man."

"His man. Never thought I'd see that."

"Me neither, but Wolf is cool."

I hummed in reply.

"You know, I used to thank God a lot when he brought Mum into Dad's life. Not only did I get someone who loved me like I was her own right from the start, but I got an annoyin' little sister."

I bit down on my bottom lip to stop the tremble before sucking in a deep breath. I wasn't sure I could handle Cody's kind words. "Cody, I'm tired."

"Then rest, sister, because I've got your back. I'll always have your back, and I'm more than fuckin' grateful God shined down on our family once again so none of us lost you."

"Cody," I choked.

He stood up, only to lean over and rest his forehead to mine. "You're my baby sister, Maya."

Tears welled and dropped. I couldn't stop them, and I didn't want to. My family had been through so much, and this, what happened to me, was so like Dad's situation.

"Cody," I cried, slamming my eyes closed.

"When we were little, Maya, you brightened my days when I was down. It was you and me against Mum and Dad for so fuckin' long. Hell, it's still like that. I'd do anythin' for you, sister, you know that.... If you weren't in my life, it'd be a fuckload duller. Glad you're here with us, Maya."

Sniffing, I wrapped my arms around him. "Love you, brother."

He made a noise in the back of his throat. "Always love you, sister."

I'd been wrong before when I'd said I would hopefully get through this. There was no hope necessary. I already knew I would because of my family.

CHAPTER SEVEN

MAYA

*I*t had been over a week since everything happened, and I'd just gotten back from John's funeral. There was an ache in my belly and chest that wouldn't leave. Seeing Moreen and their children's pain was... utterly soul breaking.

Numbly, I kicked off my heels, my back wound twinging a little, and walked to the couch to sit. Ignoring the ache, I brought my legs up and tucked my feet under me. Ruby sat next to me, scooting close to rest her head against my shoulder. My whole family had gone to John's funeral. Gratitude didn't even come close to what I felt having them at my side.

"I'll make some coffee," Mum suggested, and walked down the hall with Dad following.

Drake took the chair beside the couch Ruby and I sat on and picked up the remote. "What do you two want to watch? And it can't be some lovey-dovey movie that'll make me gag."

I managed a small laugh. "You pick."

"Action?" he asked.

"Anime," Ruby said.

"Anything, really," I told them. The tight smile I'd attempted disappeared when I remembered the bellowing cry Moreen had made when John's coffin lowered into the ground.

It still rang in my ears over and over.

With glassy eyes, I blinked to clear them and felt the tears fall.

Hadn't I cried enough?

When would I run out of tears?

They never seemed to stop over the week.

John deserved to be mourned. But even more, he deserved to be alive.

Ruby pressed herself closer into me, bringing me back. Absently, I kissed the top of her head. I glanced at the television and noticed Drake had chosen a show we'd started binging on a few days ago. A show that would usually blank my mind, but my brain didn't want to be distracted. Instead, it played the funeral over and over.

How Moreen had come to me and held me close as we both cried. How his family had all given me looks of sympathy. How I'd learned more things about John, things we wouldn't ever get to talk about. Things I couldn't tease him about and see his laugh or smile.

A knock on the door startled me, my back twinging again when I turned too fast. Drake got out of his chair, saying, "I'll get it." Drake opened the door and my stomach clenched when I saw Samuel. "Ah, hey, Mr Nareen."

"Hello, Drake, is Maya in?"

My wonderful brother glanced over his shoulder and pulled the door closed more. "She is, but it ain't a good time. The funeral was today."

"Isn't."

"What?" Drake asked.

"Now isn't a good time. No one says ain't."

Unease filled me. I didn't like Samuel correcting Drake like that.

"Right," Drake drew out. "Anyway, I'll tell my sister you stopped by."

"Thank you, and please let her know I'll call her later."

I wished he wouldn't. Like he had tried over the week. Though, I did feel a little guilty for dodging his calls and drop-bys. I just didn't want to deal with someone I hardly knew when I was in such a mess.

Drake closed the door and leaned against it. "I used to think he was cool, but, sis, you could do better."

Amusement unlocked my tense form and replaced the unease. "Thanks, Drake, I'll keep your opinion in mind."

He went back to his chair. "Seriously, I didn't realise

he had a stick wedged up his arse so much. He's never corrected me before."

"Maybe he has a lot on his mind and it slipped out," Ruby tried with a shrug. She always saw the best in people. It was sweet, and I prayed no one walked all over her for it.

Really, I couldn't be annoyed with Samuel too much. It was my fault for not speaking to him. He could just be worried for me. Yet, I didn't want his worry.

Another knock sounded, and Drake groaned as he got up and went to the door. He opened it. "Sir?"

"I forgot to pass these on. They were in the car." There was a crinkling sound, and Drake now held a bunch of flowers.

God, now I felt like a bitch.

Patting Ruby's thigh, I got to my feet when I heard a rumble of pipes. One of Dad's brothers was about to show. As far as I knew, Samuel didn't know my family was a part of a motorcycle club.

The rumble stopped when I reached the door, and Drake noticed me. My brother stepped outside and I filled the doorway.

Samuel smiled pleasantly. "Maya, it's good to see you."

"You too, Samuel. I really appreciate your concern, and the flowers, but I'm not the best company right now." Instinctively, I ran my fingers over the scab down the side of my face when his gaze snagged on it.

"I understand that."

"Yo, Drake."

My heart stilled before it gave off a giant leap.

The bike had been Texas's.

"Texas, hey," Drake replied with a beaming grin.

Texas bound up the stairs and stopped between Samuel and Drake. "What's happenin'?" He looked from Drake to Samuel, and then his gaze landed on me.

If I didn't know any better, I was sure his face softened.

Not that it mattered.

It didn't.

"Dad's inside, Texas. Go on through," I told him.

Samuel sputtered, "He's allowed in?"

Texas faced Samuel and crossed his arms over his chest.

"Samuel, he's here to see my father," I said gently. "I told you I'm not up for company right now."

The guy who I'd only been on two dates with turned his nose up at Texas before he looked back at me. "I understand, Maya. We'll speak soon. Feel better."

Feel better?

Like I was sick.

I wasn't sick.

I was heartbroken. I was sore, angry, hurt, and now annoyed.

Feel better like it was only an illness affecting me. Like I hadn't been put through a situation so devastating it would live with me for the rest of my life. I didn't even know if I'd be able to go back to work. Would I be able to trust other patients? Would I be able to work with someone else?

"Drake, give us a moment," I heard Texas say, but I was watching Samuel walk to his car while wondering what I ever saw in a man who could say "feel better" to someone after losing a person in their life who meant a lot.

He didn't know what loss was.

He didn't know so many people were broken over missing John.

He would never know what a good man John had been.

Feel better?

Really?

"Maya?"

Samuel's car drove off, and I spun to Texas. "Did you hear him?" I yelled. He nodded, arms dropping to his sides. I snorted out a humourless huff. "Feel better, like this—" I pounded on my chest as tears brimmed my eyes — "*ache* of loss is something I can fix easily with a pill." I gripped at my dress over my chest. "Like what I went through, what *John* went through was something small that could be healed in a few days. In a month." I shook my head and more tears fell. "It can't be fixed. It can't be cured. *I* lived through that. John didn't! And now... now I'll keep living through it as it repeats over and over in my head." With the heel of my palm, I tapped it against my temple again and again. "I'll keep remembering how I heard John gurgling, not knowing he was fighting for his last breath. I'll keep knowing I didn't help—" My throat closed over, and I whimpered.

"Maya, no." Texas's tone was hard and rough. I heard

him step closer. "You were fighting. It ain't your fault for John's death. It was that fuckin' cunt."

I gripped my hair, head hanging. "I-I could have done more. I could have fought harder. Injured him more to get to John."

So many different scenarios had played over and over in my mind about how I could have saved John. If only I'd been stronger, wiser, and smarter. They played over all the time.

Warm arms surrounded me, and the familiar scent of Texas invaded my senses.

"You did everything you could at the time," he whispered.

I shook my head against his chest. "I-If I did, John would be alive."

"But you could have been lost. You don't know what would have happened if you did things differently. Other people could have been around, and he might've got to them instead. If you saved John, it could have meant ten other lives were lost. You don't know, and you can't keep thinkin' what you did wasn't enough. It was, Maya. It goddamn was."

"It hurts, Texas. So much." A sob caught in my throat, and I made a whining noise. I grabbed his tee and gripped the material as my knees grew weak.

"I know, baby."

"It's not fair," I cried against him.

"It's not." He pulled me closer, holding me tighter.

"Just hold on, baby, and let it out. Don't hold anythin' in. You got people to support you, to hold you up."

So I did.

I held on and wept. Seconds or minutes later, I was swept up into his arms. I heard the front door open and Mum say, "On the couch."

With my head buried in his shoulder and neck, Texas sat with me on his lap as I cried.

"I'll take her," Dad said.

"I've got her."

"Texas, give her over."

"No offense, but she's stayin' right where she is." Arms tightened around me once more, and one slid up to cup the back of my head.

"Texas—"

"Talon, honey. Come here. Kids, kitchen please."

Footsteps sounded around me and then silence, except for the sounds I made. I wanted to stop them. I wanted to push Texas away. But everything slammed down on top of me, and I couldn't do anything but hang on and feel.

Fingers slid through my hair. "You'll be okay, baby. You will. Let it out, Maya. Give the pain to me."

I wished I could. I wished it was that easy to give it away. It wasn't. It never would be.

But I wanted to believe him that I'd be okay. It was just that in that moment, I didn't feel it. I wanted to remember when I told myself I could get through this for me, for my family, but I couldn't. Not now.

Instead, I let it out. Everything I'd been feeling. The pain I'd locked away over the week, while trying to show everyone I was strong, that I was dealing and getting through this.

I let it all out.

Until I couldn't cry anymore.

Until exhaustion took over, and sleep finally dragged me under.

CHAPTER EIGHT

MAYA

*I*t was during the following weeks after John's funeral that things started to change. Mum and Dad had sat me down a while ago and mentioned speaking to someone who specialised in traumatic experiences. At first, I hated the idea. It made me feel like my parents didn't want to deal with me. But in the end, I knew outside care could help to get me through the ordeal. I needed all the support I could get to learn to live with all that had happened without it overwhelming me.

When they also suggested to talk to Nary or Josie, I shot the idea down. I loved and trusted them, but I wanted someone outside our circle.

During the first appointment with Devlin Grey, I regretted my decision because it started as awkward as hell. He was an older man, at least in his late thirties or early forties. While he had kind eyes and a nice smile, the words were locked inside me. I didn't know if it was because he was a complete stranger or if I just didn't want to let what had happened and what I was feeling out.

"... so I killed it."

His words brought me out of my mind. "Sorry, what?" Tension locked my limbs.

"The spider my daughter was scared of."

My body unlocked, and I rested back into the chair. "Um, I wasn't really listening," I admitted.

His lips pulled up into a compassionate smile. "I know. I figured something I rambled on about would bring you back into the room." He lifted his leg and rested his calf on his other knee. "I'm wondering why the word 'kill' was what did it."

Tears brimmed as I looked to the side and out the window. I licked my dry lips before I opened my mouth to spill everything that went on that night.

"Can you fix me?" I asked after blowing my nose and wiping at my face.

"Maya, there's nothing to fix."

"But... I can't stop thinking about it. I can't stop hurting and wondering what I could have done better. I need my mind to stop... to get back to normal."

"What you were put through was traumatic, Maya. There is no easy way to deal. Something like this will play on your mind for a long time. It's how we learn to cope with those moments that matter. What you need to know, Maya, is that you did everything you could have."

He stopped when I started shaking my head. "I didn't."

"You did. You're being hard on yourself because you lost someone you care for. John's death isn't on your shoulders. You were fighting for your own life."

My gaze went back out the window.

"Maya, look at me."

Slowly, I did.

"John's death is not your fault."

Sniffing, I ran my sweaty palms down my thighs. "It feels like it is."

"It's not. There was nothing else you could have done."

I didn't want to believe him.

"Does John's wife or family blame you?"

"No."

"Does your family blame you?"

"No."

"It's not going to happen today, but one day, you will trust we're all telling you the truth."

One day, maybe I would. Devlin, which was what he preferred to be called, had made an appointment for me once a week at least for the first month. I'd been to three appointments and on the third, he'd asked about Texas because apparently, I kept bringing him up. I clamped up, not knowing what to say since I was confused about that annoying, yet sweet, man.

Texas was also something in my life that had changed.

He popped in all the time to hang out with us for no reason at all. What he was still doing in Ballarat, I didn't know. He was supposed to already have his tattoo shop set up and then left for Caroline Springs where he would run his other shop. He was supposed to be an hour away.

My gaze shifted to the man on my mind as he told my brother, "Drake, don't let little fuckers like that get to you." This was the sixth visit since the day I cried in his arms.

Not that I was counting how many times he called in.

I wasn't.

Drake sighed. "Yeah, but he just annoys the hell out of me."

"There's gonna be many people in your life who annoy you. Just learn to let shit go. Unless he says somethin' seriously bad, then you make sure you're not the one to throw the first punch, but have the last."

Drake beamed at Texas. Needless to say, my brother looked up to Texas like he did our older brother.

Rolling my eyes, I leaned back with the bowl of popcorn from the coffee table. "I don't think it's a good idea to encourage Drake to hit people."

Texas smirked. "Hey, if he's not the one who starts it, he can't get into too much trouble." He turned to Drake again. "Talon is givin' you lessons on how to hit properly, right?"

"Shit yeah. Started me two years ago."

Texas grunted and grabbed a handful of popcorn

from the bowl I'd put between us. "Good." He shoved the food into his mouth and chomped.

The front door opened, shining light into the darkened room. "Why are all the blinds down?" Ruby asked.

"Movie marathon. Texas hasn't seen any of the *Scream* movies."

"Cool." Ruby moved to the side and Dillon, Ruby's boyfriend, stepped in. "We're just going to hang in my room for a while."

"Okay. Hey, Dillon," I said.

"Hi," he replied with a small wave before Ruby took his hand and led him down the hall.

My smile turned into a wider one when I noticed Drake and Texas watching them disappear.

"Shouldn't someone keep an eye on them?" Texas asked.

"They'll be fine," I told him.

They still stared down the hall.

"Your 'rents ain't home, so maybe they should come out here and watch a movie with us?" Texas suggested.

"Nah, Ruby's probably got Dillon on the bed—" Laughter bubbled out of me when Texas and Drake stood up. "Jesus, relax you two. Ruby knows to keep her door open, and Dillon's a nice guy."

Drake snorted. "Even nice guys have dirty thoughts."

"Both of you sit down so we can start this movie." I lifted my legs and crossed them under me. Thankfully, my back had healed so the pain wasn't a constant reminder. I picked up the bowl and placed it on my lap. I managed a handful before the bowl was stolen from me by Texas.

"You gotta share, woman." He sat back down with the bowl between us again and ate some more.

"I'm just going to check something in my room," Drake said.

"Drake, sit down."

He grumbled under his breath but did sit back down. He grabbed the remote and pressed Play. I took the bowl and held it out to Drake. He shook his head and showed me a bag of lolly snakes. He loved anything gummy.

For some reason, as I thought of gummies, it reminded me of Samuel and the phone call I made to him the day after he'd popped in. I was going to do the whole "it's not you, it's me" thing in person, but I hadn't been ready to go out in public and pretend everything was all right. Samuel had taken it well. Besides, he'd already decided we weren't suited, which was for the best, because I certainly didn't even want to think about dating or a relationship with him, or anyone for that matter.

As we watched the movie, I couldn't help but take a side glance at Texas every now and then. If Cody had been living with us, I would understand why Texas kept coming around, even though he supposed to live in Melbourne. They were friends who used to hang out every chance they got. Over the years, I'd lost count of the times Dad would get a pickup call from Cody, asking him to go collect him, Texas, and Ruin after they'd gone out on the town. Now with Cody living in his own place, it didn't make sense why Texas would stop by all the time, and in a way, I kind of didn't want to think about it because....

My pulse started to race, but I refused to let my mind take me where it wanted to go. His visits meant nothing for us. Heck, maybe he wanted to become *my* friend because Cody was so busy, and Texas had decided to stick around Ballarat for a while to watch over his new business. Whatever his reason was for dropping in, it did help distract me and give me a moment of peace in my mind.

A sudden jump scare on the television had Texas nearly knocking over the popcorn bowl.

Drake started laughing. "Are you actually scared?"

"What? No way, arsehole."

"It's okay if you are, Texas," I said with a grin.

He glared at me. "Just watch the show, Maya."

We fell silent and watched more. I probably wasn't supposed to admit it, but I did like his company. Even if he was here as a friend.

"Hey, Texas," Drake started.

"Yeah? Ah fuck, he's right there," he yelled at the movie.

Drake chuckled. "I heard Dad say you're now livin' in Ballarat."

I froze, a handful of popcorn halfway to my mouth.

"You heard right."

"That's wicked, man. You gonna run your tattoo shop?"

"That's the plan. Why, you lookin' for some ink?"

I spluttered over the shock to quickly say, "Not yet."

Texas and Drake snickered, their attention going back to the show, but I couldn't stop thinking about Texas actually *living* in Ballarat. Like, permanently. Why would he want to change? He had another shop in Melbourne. Wouldn't he stay where his family was? When did he decide this? *Why* did he decide it? Was it because he couldn't find a manager in Ballarat? That could be it. I wondered what Dodge and Low thought of his choice.

Did it mean he would be hanging out more often?

That could explain why he was here in the first place. Like I'd thought, Cody was busy with work and Channa. Texas could be bored.... No, wait, he had a business to run. Why wasn't he there now?

"How is the new shop going?" I asked, shifting on the couch to see him better.

"Good. It's pickin' up."

Then why was he here? It was Saturday. Wouldn't it be a busy day?

"You must be busy, then?"

He shrugged. "Not too bad. I can take on clients when I want."

Oh.

Did that mean he just didn't have any that day?

"Would you employ me when I'm older?" Drake asked.

"So you can have only female clients?" I teased. Drake loved being loved by women. He definitely got attention from them, since he looked like his father, and Mum said women chased Dad all the time. Even after they saw he wore a wedding ring.

Drake's radiant smile said it all. "Maybe."

Texas and I laughed, then he asked, "How are you with drawin'?"

Drake shrugged. "Not bad."

I pointed at him. "That's a lie." I turned to Texas. "He's amazing, like Ruby. You should see some of his work."

Texas nodded. "I'd like to."

"Go grab some," I encouraged. Drake bolted out of the room.

A few moments later, we heard Ruby yell, "Get out, Drake."

"Quit kissin' my sister," Drake boomed.

"Oh shit," I muttered and went to stand up until Texas gripped my wrist.

"Get out!" Ruby screamed.

"Yo, Drake, grab your stuff already," Texas called, and we heard pounding footsteps.

"Thanks," I said, leaning back into the couch.

"No problem, but I still think it'd be good to get Ruby and her fella out here."

Snorting, I shook my head. "Why? Because they're kissing?"

"Because I remember bein' his age, and there was one thing on my mind."

Rolling my eyes, I went to cross my arms over my chest but noticed Texas still held my wrist. He released it at my movement. My skin was still warm from his touch. "Like all boys, but Dillon wouldn't disrespect Ruby in any way."

"You trust him?"

"Yes, I do."

"Then that's enough for me."

When Drake ran back into the room, Texas looked away from me and at the drawings Drake placed on the coffee table. I studied Texas while they talked. What did he mean by my trusting Dillon was enough for him?

Not that it mattered. Just like how I could still feel his handprint on my wrist.

None of it mattered because I wouldn't let it.

I wouldn't think of his kindness as anything other than a growing friendship.

I would ignore his attractiveness, his ink-covered skin, his smirks, grins, and laughs.

I'd place him in the friendship zone because that was all it would ever be.

A scream burst out of the television, causing me to jump.

Blood.

Everywhere.

There'd been so much in the ambulance, and the sounds John had made while he... while he....

"Drake, turn off the TV."

"Fuck," I heard my brother say.

Blinking, I felt the wetness on my cheeks and quickly

wiped at them. "Sorry," I whispered into the now quiet room.

"Don't apologise," Drake ordered before he picked up his artwork and stormed out of the room.

Wincing, I glanced at Texas. The only light was the one that Drake must have turned on at some point, but I'd been lost in my head. "I didn't mean to—"

Texas shifted closer, the popcorn bowl squished between us, and cupped the side of my face. "Like Drake said, don't apologise, Maya. There's gonna be many more times when you get lost in your head. Everyone knows this, and everyone knows what you went through. Let it happen, and let the people around you help you through it."

My bottom lip trembled. "Shut up. Don't say nice things. Not now. Not unless you want me to be a blubbering mess again," I whispered, looking down into the bowl. My erratic heart was yelling at me to kiss him for being so nice. Thank God my brain was at least smarter and kept my body locked where it was.

Texas chuckled. "All right, baby. I'll shut up, but know I don't mind when you're a blubbering mess."

Groaning, I shook my head and gave him a feeble smile. I shifted back enough for him to drop his hand.

Friends.

Just friends.

And that was okay. I loved the friends I already had, but I could always do with one more.

CHAPTER NINE

TEXAS

J had a feeling Maya had friend zoned me. But that was all right. She wasn't near ready for my confession of the future I saw for us. I was also enjoying the time we'd been spending together. It was terrible to say, but I fucking loved that I'd had the chance to be there for her when she'd crashed over everything. When that prick's words had set her off. I loved it because if I hadn't had that chance, I doubted she'd have given me the time of day. She'd still be dodging me every time I was around. Now, I could tell she didn't mind my company.

The day I'd seen her at Coyote's business, I ruffled her hair, which I was sure caused her to leave. Coyote had called me a fucking idiot. At first, I didn't know why, until I'd asked him just the other day about it, and he'd explained that she would have taken that as a brotherly or friendly pat. I could have fucking knocked myself out for it. I'd only done it because I'd wanted to touch her in some way.

Since then, I'd made sure not to do it again. I didn't want her to get that impression from me. When the time did come, I couldn't have her say I treated her in a "my friend's sister" way or anything.

She'd have to see the difference, wouldn't she?

I'd hoped to Christ she did, because I was enamoured by her.

She'd always been a bright spot in a gathering—smiling, laughing, and sharing her love around the room. Yet, if she was pissed at something, she'd let you know. She got fiery when protecting those she cared for. Admittedly, when my infatuation started, I stalked the shit out of her, just for a glance or a word from her. What helped was how our families were close.

Christ, I sounded like a creep.

Did she still see something in me?

Could the crush she'd had when she was younger still be there under the surface?

Fuck, I hoped to Christ it was.

Hoped that I hadn't screwed it up by acting like a dick around her, by unconsciously flaunting my exes around her.

A throat cleared. I looked up from tattooing my client's shoulder to see Dodge standing in the doorway.

"Yo, old man."

"Shut it, kid. We've got the rest of your stuff. Give me the keys, and I'll start shifting it in."

I waved towards the bench in the corner. "They're on there. I'm nearly done here, which I'm sure Nick is grateful for."

"Hell yes," Nick said with a grimace. He'd been sitting there for four hours already.

Chuckling, I went back to work on the last of the shading. "Give me five," I told Dodge.

"You got it." He walked out of the room.

"That your dad?" Nick asked and then hissed.

"He's my uncle, but he's been around since I was fourteen, so yeah, he's also my dad."

I caught Nick's wicked grin. "He's hot."

Chuckling, I shook my head. "I'll let him know. But you might want to run if his woman hears about it. She's possessive as fuck."

"Then maybe keep it to yourself or at least wait until I'm far away from the shop."

Snorting, I wiped over the tattoo. "I'll give you a head start."

"Thanks."

Tipping my chin towards the mirror, I told him, "Go check it out before I wrap it."

He climbed off the table and stood in front of the mirror, shifting slightly to the left and right. The bright smile and happy eyes were what I loved about this job. People wanted my work. They loved my designs, and it meant so goddamn much that clients were waiting and willing to have my ink on them.

"Man, this is the fucking best. Damn lucky you moved here."

"Glad you trusted my work to put it on you."

"Just wait, you're gonna be sought after. I give it another month, and you'll have bookings coming out of your ears."

Chuckling, I shrugged, feeling a little bashful at the damn praises. Though, word was already starting to get around, and the shop was picking up enough that I'd have to employ a third artist soon. Also, the girl who took care of the bookings was finalising her piercing course and taking up a room here for it, so I'd need to find another front person.

"Thanks, man." I wrapped his ink and gave him the instructions on how to take care of it. Nick headed out to pay at the front desk with Monnie. Nick had been the last client for the day, so after I cleaned up, I made my way towards the front of the store.

"Texas, that dude has a hard-on for you."

Grinning, I shrugged. "As long as he comes back for more work, I don't mind."

"That's true. Now, before you leave, you know your schedule for tomorrow?"

"Yep. I'm working on the artwork for Josh's tonight. The rest are already done. You'll lock up after Hex is done with his client?"

She winked. "You know it."

"Thanks, Mon, have a good night. Later, Hex," I yelled back down the hall.

His reply was quick. "Later."

I was beyond grateful for Monnie and Hex. Both had followed me down from my Melbourne store to work hereafter I'd begged them to and found their replacements. Besides, they'd always been talking about moving to the country, and when I'd offered, they'd jumped at the chance. The only thing keeping them in Melbourne for now was their lease, which they couldn't get out of. Luckily, it was up in three weeks. When Monnie wasn't busy with work and her course, she was searching for places for them to live.

Stepping outside, I noticed the sun had started to set. I had about half an hour to help Dodge with the rest of my shit in the daylight. Daylight savings sucked. Turning, I walked to the right of the shop where my house was attached and entered. I'd been damn lucky the house went up for sale after I'd bought the shop connected to it. Even if the house was a bit outdated compared to the shop, I was looking forward to doing it up.

"Honey, I'm home," I called after entering and closing the front door.

"In the kitchen," Low answered.

As I made my way down the hall, I glanced into my bedroom, which was already set up. Next was the spare room that I'd turn into an office, and nearing the living room, there were two other bedrooms. The place was big, and it would probably take me most of my life to pay it off, but it'd be worth it. When I saw the space the house had, my first thought was of my future and how it'd be perfect for when I had my woman and kids in it with me, making it a home.

At the back of the house was the large open-plan living, dining, and kitchen area where a family, one I'd make, would spend the majority of the time.

As soon as I entered, Low turned to me with her hands on her hips. "Are you sure this is what you want?"

Chuckling, I approached and gave her a hug. "Bit late for me to back out now." With a kiss to the top of her head, I went to grab a beer out of the refrigerator. "Want one?"

"No thanks, and also no, it's not too late to back out."

"Low, I've already made the down payment, got the shop set up, and now moved in. I'd call that too late."

Her nose scrunched up. "Just know you can come home whenever you want. You can put this place up for rent." She wasn't yet used to the idea of me being an hour away, and still a little peeved that I hadn't told her anything until after I'd signed the contract to the house. Dodge knew. He'd helped me with the banks and an early settlement, but we'd known it was best to hold off on telling Low because she'd have her back up about me moving from Melbourne.

"It's not far, Low," I told her for what felt like the millionth time.

She grumbled under her breath, "Fine."

Shifting back her way, I curled an arm around her

shoulders and gently rocked her into my side. "Love you, Low."

"Yeah, yeah. Get out the back and help my man bring in the couch."

"Couch? Low, I was gonna get a couch soon."

"You can't sit in lawn chairs, Texas."

Sighing, I dropped my head back to look for patience. It wasn't there. "Low, you guys have already done enough—"

She waved me off and went back to unpacking crockery I didn't fucking own. "I don't want to hear it."

"And I suppose you don't want to talk about the shit I know you're sneaking into my cupboards?"

"Exactly."

I groaned. "Low—"

"Can't hear you, but I do hear Trey callin' for you. Shoo."

Scrubbing a hand over my face, I walked out the back where a damn moving truck was parked. I went to the rear and found Dodge in the back.

"What the fuck, Dodge?"

He chuckled as he faced me. "I'd take on anyone but my woman, kid. Let's just say she got her way."

"I'm payin' you back."

He scowled. "Fuck off, you are."

"Dodge, I don't want handouts."

"Kid, this ain't a handout. This is a future investment. Look after us when we're old or pay for the retirement village when the time comes. Just make it a damn good one. If you don't like that suggestion, pay us back when this shop gets on its feet like I know it will."

He knew I couldn't argue with any of that. "All right."

He grinned. "Good. Now get in here and help me before we run outta light."

We worked on getting everything from the van, and the chore led us into the dark, since I now owned a new table and chairs, couch, lounge chair, computer desk, bookcase, coffee table, and a spare bed. Low explained the guest queen-size bed was for her and Dodge to sleep in when they visited, or for Rommy, my sister, when she wanted to come see me. Rommy had already texted me and told me she was coming down for a weekend soon. She couldn't make it now because she had work at the garage. Rommy didn't do her VCE to get her certificate of education by going into exams at the end of year twelve. Instead, she went into VCAL, which was a part-time hands-on option for students in year eleven and twelve that would lead her to her apprenticeship in the garage at the compound. She'd been fascinated by the way cars and bikes worked, and Dodge was more than happy to take her on because she was a quick study for it all.

Low ordered pizza for dinner, and I at least got to the front door to pay for it when it arrived. Taking the pizza back into the kitchen, I placed the boxes on the clean bench, since Low had been crazy with tidying, and got out a couple of beers.

"Low?" I asked.

"I'm good."

I passed the other one to Dodge and grabbed Low a soda. Dodge stayed leaning against the counter opposite where Low and I sat at the counter seats. I didn't realise how damn hungry I was until I'd gulped down four slices.

"When's Talon lookin' at addin' you to the club?"

Swallowing my bite, I told Dodge, "Not next weekend, but the one after. Wants to do it at the family barbeque day."

"Lucky you don't have to join as a prospect," Low said. "Dodge told me the crappy jobs he had to do."

"Yeah, you punk. Now I can't make your life hell." Dodge smirked.

"You already do, old man."

He shot me the middle finger. "But seriously, you know you don't have to be a member to be family. You already are."

"I know. I held off because my apprenticeship kept me busy, then there was branching out into my own business, but now that I'm settled, it's time to become Hawks." I glanced away and shrugged. "Besides, I've always looked up to you and want to follow in your footsteps in some way."

"Jesus, kid, you just hit me in the damn heart."

"Translation, he loves you," Low put in.

"He knows that," Dodge grumbled, probably as uncomfortable as I was with this feelings shit.

"I do."

"Well, looks like we'll be back in Ballarat in a couple of weeks."

"You don't have to come," I told them.

Low punched me in the arm. "We wouldn't miss it." When she rested her elbow on the counter and head in her palm to stare at me, I knew something was up.

"What?" I asked around a mouthful of slice.

"You ever gonna be honest and just straight up tell me who brought you to Ballarat?"

She caught my gaze flaring. I opened my mouth, closed it, and fought not to look at Dodge. Had he said something? I'd asked him not to because we both knew that once one of the pussy posse members knew some gossip, the rest would hear it within hours.

Low glared and pointed at my face. "So, there is someone. I've had my suspicions, and I knew you wouldn't just up and leave the family for no reason other than opening another shop, but you could have done that in Melbourne. Who is it? Are you gonna tell me now? Is it someone I know? I bet it is. Why else wouldn't you want me to know?"

"Jesus, woman." Dodge chuckled. "Take a breath."

Her glare was back and aimed at her man. "Don't you "woman" me, Trey. You obviously know. I don't understand why I couldn't know. I wouldn't have been such a pain about you moving if I knew—"

Both Dodge and I rose our brows at her.

She rolled her eyes. "Okay, I wouldn't have been as bad as I have been. I still would have tried to stop it because you're one of our babies."

It really did suck that Dodge and Low couldn't have

kids. They'd told us enough times we were enough for them, but they would have been fucking brilliant parents to their own like they were with Rommy and me after we moved in with Dodge when his sister, our mum, died.

"Low, I told you already today. Love you. You've been the best mum to Rommy and me."

Tears welled in her eyes. She swiped at them and scowled. She hated showing emotions.

"And havin' grown up around you and your girl-friends, I knew if I'd told you, the rest of your girls would know in seconds." I couldn't risk anything getting back to Maya. She wasn't ready for what I saw us as.

She scoffed. "I know how to keep secrets."

"Little bird" was all Dodge said.

"Sometimes," she added with another glare at Dodge. "Do you really not want me to know?"

I rubbed a hand over my beard. "Can you wait just a little longer?"

She sighed. "Fine. Even though I've already guessed, but I was waiting for you to admit it. I suppose I'll just wait until you and Maya are datin'."

"How...?"

She grinned, but it vanished all too quickly. "You were wrecked when Maya nearly died. I was at the hospital, Texas. I felt and saw your pain. A man who wasn't half in love with someone wouldn't have reacted that way. I get why you didn't tell me. Us bitches talk. We really do."

Did that mean she'd already talked with her girls about this? Was that why Zara had come up to me outside the hospital? I'd always wondered. I'd just never approached her about it. Low's next words brought me out of my thoughts.

"But I also know you gotta go slow with that girl. She is something special, and even though you're my own kid, I will fuck you up if you hurt her. She's been through enough. And shit, she's been into you since she was sixteen. Ever since then, I witnessed her hurt when you had other women on your arm."

I went to explain that I hadn't seen what was in front of me, but her hand resting on my arm shut me up.

"Boy, I didn't say anything back then because I knew you had to sort your own life out and that eventually you'd wake up to see what was in front of you."

Clenching my jaw, I nodded. I didn't know what to say. I felt like my gut had been kicked for not trusting Low with this.

She patted my hand. "I'm not mad you didn't tell me, so don't stress about it. I haven't said anything about my suspicions, which were right," she said pointedly, "to anyone, and I won't. I just wanted you to know that I'm in your corner, and I hope Maya will see what an awesome man you've grown into."

My throat thickened. "Thanks, Low."

She waved me off. "Still, you can come home anytime you want."

Smiling, I hugged her close. I was damn lucky to have them in my life.

CHAPTER TEN

MAYA

*D*ad wasn't talking to me.

A couple of days ago, after a visit from Swan, who was more like a sister to me than a friend, I'd gone to my parents and announced I was taking a trip to get away from everything.

They were shocked, since I'd never hinted at wanting to travel to begin with, but Swan had mentioned that since she was turning eighteen in a couple of days, she'd been considering getting away from the cold winter to some sunny days in Queensland. When she'd mentioned she was going to beg her parents to go, I'd blurted that I was interested in a trip.

Dad flat-out refused to let me go and stormed from the room. Mum had laid her hand on my arm and told me she'd talk to him. Unlike Dad, she believed a couple of weeks away could do me good. It wasn't like I actually *needed* his permission, since I was twenty-one, but I *wanted* it out of respect for the way he protected his family. In a way, Dad was like a mafia boss in how it would make my life easier if I got his permission to begin with. I also didn't want him to worry after everything we'd all been through.

If Dad gave in, I knew there would be strict instructions I would have to follow, and I'd do it to keep him happy, and to also ensure he didn't send one of his brothers after us to keep an eye out. So, I kept my fingers crossed that Mum would persuade Dad. Besides, Queensland wasn't far away, and Swan wasn't like any of my other friends who liked to party and get into trouble.

The time away would be good to clear my mind. To help me work out what I wanted and where my next move would be. I still hadn't made up my mind about work. The thought of going back had my throat closing over and my body shaky. My therapist had told me not to rush my decision. Even my boss said the same.

I wished I knew.

I did.

But I didn't, and not knowing was frustrating me.

Sighing, I excused myself from the conversation Ivy had started with Mally and me and went to get myself a drink. We were at the compound for the family barbeque day, and usually I loved being around everyone to catch up on what they had all been up to, but I wasn't feeling the crowd right now.

A headache pounded at my temples. It wasn't because of the company. I loved everyone here, but I just wasn't in the mood to be around so many.

Once outside, I made my way over to Texas, who sat beside Dodge. I couldn't help but smile about how I used to steer clear of Texas at any event. Always afraid I'd make a fool of myself or that my attraction to him would grow more.

Now, after having been around him a lot lately, I could admit my attraction had grown, but it had nothing to do with his good looks and a lot to do with the person he was.

Honestly, I'd been a fool to let my crush on him infringe on a friendship that I knew was growing between us.

"Hey," I called once I was close.

They both looked my way and grinned. Dodge stood up and hugged me close. "I was just about to go grab a beer. You want anythin', darlin'?" he asked.

"I'm good. Thanks, though."

He winked down at me and took off towards his woman who sat near the drink table.

Looking back at Texas, I said, "I didn't catch you inside. I wanted to say congrats on becoming Hawks." Texas had just been brought into the club as a member. He now wore a club vest. Only like Dad, and a couple of other brothers, he'd kept his real name for the patch on his vest. When I'd asked him if he was worried about the possibility that he'd get appointed a terrible club name, he'd laughed and told me he'd already spoken to Dad about keeping Texas as his member name as well. Dad and the brothers had voted and had been fine with it.

"Thanks, babe. Come take a seat." He nodded down at the chair Dodge had vacated.

I lowered myself into the seat as he drank the rest of his beer down and placed it on the ground. "So," I drew out, "how's it feel, being a full member now?"

He snorted. "Like nothin' changed. Hawks has always been in my blood."

Nodding, I leaned back in the chair more and tipped my face up to the sun, closing my eyes. It was one of those rare sunny days in winter, which was lucky. "I can understand that." I turned my head and found his gaze already on me. My stomach fluttered to life. *Shit.* Straightening, I rested my cooler hands on my cheeks as I leaned forward with my elbows on my thighs.

"Ruby and Drake on holidays now?" Texas asked.

Random talk, I could do that and ignore the butterflies that had come to life even more so the last few times I'd been around Texas. Also, ignoring them would benefit me more as it meant I could keep this new friendship. A friendship I liked. Yes, I had my girlfriends I could hang out with, but I enjoyed the visits from Texas. There was also the chance he probably needed this friendship, since his other brothers were busy with their better halves.

I nodded. "Friday was their last day. Now it'll be two

weeks of gaming for Drake and reading for Ruby. That's when she's not glued to her boyfriend."

Texas chuckled. "I'll have to come by and check out Drake's games. Haven't played in years."

"But you used to?"

"Hell yes. I was fuckin' awesome."

"What made you stop?"

"Life, drawing, apprenticeship, work. But now that I run my own businesses, I can pick and choose the hours I want to do."

"But aren't you busy?"

"I am." He smirked. "But I also have employees. It makes me able to get picky on the clients."

"Are there some clients you won't take on?"

He nodded. "Yeah, I know my skills and where I'd show my best work."

"What are those?"

"This fucker is good at any design," Ruin said as he bent to kiss my temple. "Hey, girl."

I had to shield my eyes from the sun when I tipped my head back to see him. "Ruin, where's your better half?"

He snorted and nodded off to the side. "Stuck with Mum and her posse."

Wolf stood in the middle of Mally, Ruin's mum, Deanna, which was never good, Ivy, and Josie. The last was the only saving grace in that group. She'd have Wolf's back if needed.

Texas chuckled. "You're a fuckin' cruel man, brother."

Ruin joined in laughing and shrugged. He glanced over just when Wolf looked our way with a deathly glare.

"He's going to kick your butt later," I told him.

"He can try." His grin turned wicked.

Rolling my eyes, I smacked his arm. "Get your mind out of the gutter."

"Ha, too late." He pulled up another chair to my other side and sat. "Now, what's this bullshit you were sayin', brother? Your skills let you do any type of design. I've seen all your work."

"I might be good, but if it's somethin' I hate doin', like roses and butterflies, I don't get enjoyment outta it. I want to love what I create, and I reckon it helps the clients to fall in love with it as well."

I could understand that. He wanted to keep feeling the passion about his work. Still, I couldn't help but tease, "Damn, and here I was thinking about getting you to do a butterfly and rose on me."

I thought he would have laughed. He didn't. Instead, his intense gaze had me swallowing thickly, and the fluttering came to life in my belly. "Babe, I'd do anythin' you wanted."

Our gazes held.

I needed to look away. I needed a distraction. Those words were beginning to mean more than he intended.

"Do I need to leave?" Ruin asked.

Blinking, I forced a small laugh. "No. What are you talking about?" I snorted. "Leave? What for? You're being weird." *Jesus, shut up, Maya.*

Ruin scoffed, his brows high. "Yeah, okay."

Someone stepped up to our small group, thankfully. Wolf glowered down at his man.

"Babe, what took you so long?" Ruin stood up with a smug grin. "Here, take my seat."

Wolf crossed his arms over his chest. "You left me to fend for myself all because I refused to suck your cock on the way here?"

Beer spewed out of Texas's mouth, and he started coughing while I cackled. Texas hit his chest over and over as he hacked up a lung.

Ruin scowled, placing his hands on his hips. "No, babe. I left you standing over there because you told Link and Ryo about... what happened in the bathroom."

Now I wanted to know what happened.

Wolf grinned. "How many times do I have to tell you? People expel gas all the time. There's nothing to be upset about."

Okay, I could have done without knowing.

Texas snorted through his laugh, and I had to cover my mouth to hide mine.

Ruin glared down at us before he waved a hand our way. "Great, babe. Now these two know."

"Brother, people fart. There ain't anythin' to be embarrassed about," Texas said. "Lucky you didn't shit yourself in front of your man."

Ruin ground his teeth together. "It wasn't Wolf in the bathroom."

"What?" I laughed. "Who was it?"

Wolf opened his mouth, but Ruin was there, covering it with his hand. "Don't you dare," he warned his partner. "Let's just say it was someone important in the family and leave it at that, but you two aren't to breathe a damn word of it to anyone." He dropped his hand to take a grip of Wolf's wrist. "We're gonna get a drink."

After they'd walked off, Texas snorted. "Bet Ruin won't leave Wolf with the women again."

Grinning, I nodded. "He's learned his lesson. Though, I got more enjoyment out of your reaction than anything."

"Shut it," he mumbled.

"Maya," I heard Mum call before I spotted her walking through the throngs of people with Swan at her side. Mum's smile was cheerful, like she'd just found out something good and just had to share. "There you are. Hey, Texas."

"Wildcat." It was what the brothers of the club called her. "Swan."

Swan raised her hand close to her belly and waved at Texas. "Hi," she said meekly. She'd admitted to me once that she thought Texas was hot. Not that she'd ever do anything about any type of attraction with anyone. She was too shy and timid. Always had been, even with a mother who was outspoken and loud. Not that Deanna was her biological mother.

"I have good news," Mum announced.

"What?"

"Your father finally said yes."

My eyes widened, and I straightened in my seat. "Shut. Up. He did not."

Swan nodded. "Zara just told my parents. It's set."

Standing up, I gripped her hands to raise them in the air and cheered. "Hell yes."

"What's this?" Texas asked, and I turned to see him standing behind me.

Beaming, I told him, "Dad finally agreed to let me go with Swan to Queensland for a couple of weeks."

Texas's grin faded. "Alone?"

We quieted and I narrowed my gaze at him. "Swan and I will have each other."

His lips thinned as he peered over at us, but then his attention went to Mum. "You sure the prez agreed?"

Mum smothered her smile by wiping a hand over her mouth. "Yes, Texas." I wasn't sure what had her smiling because it wasn't the reaction building in me. Annoyance surfaced. I was sick of Texas acting like an overprotective brother.

"Maya!" Speaking of brothers, Cody stormed our way. His gaze snapped to Mum. "Mum, you can't be serious about lettin' her go to Queensland."

I groaned. "Cody, I'm freaking twenty-one years old. I can do want I want. You don't see Griz stopping Swan going."

Sometimes, I wanted to kick the shit out of the men in my life.

"Never said I was happy about it, though," Griz put in from somewhere.

"Maya." My brother's tone softened. "Come on, sis. You'll be states away without any of us at your back, and after everything...."

I jutted my chin up. "After everything, you would think my brother would support me having some time away to enjoy life."

He sighed and ran a hand over the back of his neck.

Stepping close to him, I wrapped my arms around his waist. "Thank you for caring, for being worried, but I *need* this, Cody. I do."

"Fine."

Grinning up at him, I said, "Thank you."

I still couldn't believe Dad had agreed, but I really did think this trip would be good for me.

CHAPTER ELEVEN

TEXAS

*E*ven though I'd wanted to go to Talon and tell him it was a mistake to let Maya go, I didn't. What she'd said to her brother that day, about needing this time away, had me keeping my mouth shut and my fear to myself. But fuck, did I miss her. I was used to knowing she was at home where I could drop in whenever I wanted to see her.

I picked up my phone and scrolled through our texts.

The morning she left, I sent her a message telling her to have fun but stay safe.

She'd shot back an eye-roll emoji, saying that she would. I'd then wanted to leave her alone, let her have her time away without any of the men in her life hounding her.

I'd lasted until that afternoon.

ME:

How was the flight?

I'd already known she'd landed safely from her Snapchat stories.

MAYA:

Good. We're relaxing by the pool right now since it's still warm for us Victorians at 5pm.

Along with words, she'd sent a photo of her legs. I had gripped my phone to a point of it near cracking when I'd wondered who else was there seeing those damn stunning, smooth limbs.

ME:

You should get a blanket in case it gets cold.

There'd been a long pause after I'd sent it.

MAYA:

We'll be heading in soon before it gets too dark.

I winced and didn't bother replying in case I went all

caveman on her and demanded to know who was around or what she was wearing on the top half.

The texts became a ritual. What surprised me more was when my phone buzzed and it was Maya. It had almost been a week since she'd been gone, but for once, she reached out to me first.

I smiled even before reading the text. Not even giving a shit that I loved she was thinking about me.

MAYA:

> Is it hard to believe I actually miss home?

ME:

Not at all. I hate the heat over there.

MAYA:

> I think that's what I'm feeling. I'm used to the cold winters. Still, I'm having fun. We went to a theme park today. Swan and I discovered we don't like rollercoasters.

ME:

Did anyone puke?

MAYA:

> No, thank God. How's work?

ME:

Busy. I got to ink this today.

I followed up with a picture of Gojo, an anime character off *Jujutsu Kaisen*.

I grinned at Maya's instant reply.

OMG that is epic. Seriously, Texas, I love it. One day I'm dropping into your work and checking out more designs.

ME:

Deal. I'll look forward to it.

MAYA:

I'm still looking at the picture. It's amazing. But what I don't understand is why you chose to live in Ballarat over Melbourne. You'd have more business in the city, wouldn't you?

My heart skipped a beat over the truth of it.

Was it crazy and stalkerish that I'd moved to Ballarat for her... without her even knowing?

Fuck. Probably. And it wasn't like she was ready to hear the truth. Shit, maybe I could never tell her the real reason or else she'd think I was a creep.

ME:

I've always enjoyed coming to Ballarat, the quietness of it. Melbourne's too cramped. Too chaotic. The country's always appealed to me.

MAYA:

I can completely understand that. But don't you miss it even a little? Miss your family being close?

ME:

Not at all with the city. And I see the family enough and they're not far away.

MAYA:

True. Anyway, what are you going to do for your Saturday night?

ME:

What I'm doing now. Sitting in my living room drawing, and watching Die Hard.

MAYA:

Bruce Willis is a legend. But I thought you'd be heading to the clubhouse at least.

ME:

> Nah, not feeling it. You going out drinking?

She threw back at me:

> Nah, not feeling it

Followed immediately by another text.

> Swan and I are sitting by the pool for a while and then we're thinking of going to the movies. Sounds lame, I know.

ME:

> Not at all. Hell, I'm home on my own.

MAYA:

> LOL. I'm surprised you don't have anyone there with you.

She still thought I was after someone to just warm my bed.

ME:

> Not interested.

MAYA:

> Um, okay? Anyway, we're about to go. TTYL.

ME:

Later.

After that, the days seemed to drag, though it was lucky that work was always entertaining. But I still couldn't wait for the night. For when we'd text more. We talked about random things, work, life, music, and movies. What I liked most about her texts was knowing that I was on her mind.

Only there was a small problem with us being in contact all the time. Well, not small. But when Maya was constantly on my mind, my dick was hard half the time.

I placed my phone on the couch and glanced down to see the tent in my grey tracksuit pants. Palming my hard-on, I squeezed. A thrill shot through me.

Fuck.

Clenching my jaw, I scooted my arse down a little and tugged the front of my pants down, gripping my hardness. Closing my eyes, I pumped my hand over my dick and brought up an image of Maya sitting close to me on the couch but not touching. However, her eyes were drinking me in as I jerked off.

For her, I'd run my warm, tattooed hand up and down my cock at a fast pace, like I was doing on my own, with the tip already leaking. In my imagination, Maya's breathing would accelerate, pushing her tits up and down, and slowly, she'd run her hands over them, teasing me with a pinch to her nipples.

Christ.

I wished she was here. Wished she was watching. I wanted to see the desire in her eyes, the way she wouldn't be able to control herself by sliding a hand into her panties to touch—

"Shit," I hissed as my cum erupted and landed on my bare chest.

Panting, I looked down at the mess I'd made while thinking, hoping I didn't embarrass myself when I did have the chance to have Maya in front of me in that way.

CHAPTER TWELVE

MAYA

J nibbled on my thumbnail as I stared down at my phone. Texas and I had been messaging, and sometimes calling, each other since I'd left. I liked talking with him. But I couldn't help but wonder if he minded that it was his friend's sister taking up his time, and if I annoyed him with the randomness of our conversations.

But he messaged you first.

He had.

I glanced up when Swan approached with our cocktails. Smiling, I reached up and took the drink she'd held out.

"Thanks. What's this one called?" We'd been trying different ones each night.

"Manhattan." She sat on the lounge chair next to me at the pool's edge.

We both took a sip. My nose screwed up, and I peered at Swan to see she'd had the same reaction. We laughed.

"Not my favourite," Swan said.

"Mine neither." Yet we wouldn't waste it. It wasn't the first drink we'd manage to finish when we didn't like it. "I know I've said it before, but thank you for allowing me to tag along on your time away."

"Maya, no offense to my family, but I'd rather have your company than theirs on a trip. There's also the fact that the thought of going alone was overwhelming. If anything, you're doing me a favour by coming. You know I love spending time with you."

"Same." Even with the three-year age difference, Swan and I had always gotten along. My phone chimed and I glanced down at my lap, seeing there was a new message from Texas.

See, he messaged you.

Swan hummed. "Just pointing it out, but you smile every time he texts."

I scoffed. "I do not."

"You do. It's sweet and good to see you two finally talking."

"Honestly, I wished I'd never let my crush get in the way. We'd have been friends from the start if I hadn't." At least I hoped so. I also wished Cody had gotten one of his other friends to be my first kiss. Then maybe I wouldn't have turned into an obsessed fool who thought love could come from a first kiss. I wouldn't have become annoyed and frustrated with Texas when he didn't see me as anything but his friend's sister.

"Do you still like him?" Swan asked.

Yes was my instant thought. How could I not? The more I got to know him, the more there was to like.

I glanced off over the pool. "Yeah, but now I know my feelings aren't, and never will be, reciprocated, and I'm... well, most of the time I'm okay with that. I like the friendship we've built."

Looking back at Swan, I saw that her lips had thinned.

"What?" I asked.

She shook her head. "Nothing."

"Swan, I know you, and you're holding back about something. Is all this talk making you think of Lockland?" She'd been heartbroken when her best friend, who was now a singing superstar, had left town to further his career. However, he left before she even realised how deep her feelings went for him. How much she'd loved him. When she'd worked out what Lockland meant to her, she still said nothing, even when in the first couple of years they kept in contact. Not that she'd admit it, but she stayed silent because she didn't want to be the person who could come between him and stardom. I expected she was afraid of being rejected.

She picked at some lint on her shorts. "No, it's not that."

"Then what?"

She bit her bottom lip, glanced at me, and then away. "I'm not sure if I should say anything."

Sitting up, I planted my feet on the ground and placed my drink down. "Oh, now you have to tell me."

She copied my position, and my stomach dipped when she took my hands in hers. "Does Texas mean a lot to you?"

Another dip to my belly, like it was on its own trip over a bumpy road.

Did Texas mean a lot to me?

Wait, why was she asking in the first place?

Her hands tightened around mine. "Maya?"

Right, Texas.

Glancing at the ground, I thought of him, and like always lately, it brought a smile to my face.

I wouldn't lie. It was time to admit, even to myself, that my crush grew wings and had taken off in flight.

Did Texas mean a lot to me? Yes, he definitely did. I wasn't sure if I could live with only a friendship, but I really wanted to try. I wanted to keep Texas around. I'd definitely messed up when I'd dodged him instead of getting to know him.

"Yeah, he does."

A slow, soft smile grew on Swan's lips. "Good."

A small laugh left me. "Why?"

"Don't you think it's strange that since what happened to you, Texas has been dropping by your house all the time?"

I pulled back, a little surprised we were talking about

this. "Well, I mean, he's new to living in Ballarat. With Dad being president, of course he'll want to see him. Also, Cody's always busy with Channa. And with Ruin in Melbourne, he's not really close to the other brothers his age yet. I guess he's after someone new to hang out with."

She smirked. "I can see you've already thought about it."

I snorted. "Of course I have."

"Okay then, think about this; he doesn't need friends his own age because when you're in the club, *all* the brothers are his friends and family. He's close with all of them, no matter the age. Does he even see Talon when he's over?"

I had to think about it for a moment. "Dad's busy. He's not always around."

"Yet Texas knows when you're at home."

"He... asks." I hadn't pondered on that fact, not wanting to grab hold of how sweet his visiting was. Now that it was voiced and pretty much spelled out for me, could it be true? Did I dare imagine his visits were just for me? Just to *see* me.

"Maya." Her hands tightened around mine once again. "Dad was there that night."

I stilled. "I... I know." I remembered looking out over the group. My gaze had even flicked over Texas. But why was she bringing this up now?

"I overheard him talking to Mum about something that he saw."

"What?" I whispered.

"The way Texas reacted."

"Sorry?" I asked quickly, wanting to understand, wanting her to get to the point.

"Maya." Her tone was soft and knowing. "Texas lost it. Dad had never seen him like that. At the scene, he wanted to get to you. Wanted to help you. He shut down when... when everyone thought they lost you."

An invisible force wrapped around my chest and pressed. "What?" I breathed.

Swan nodded. "He'd been on his knees when Dad got him to his feet and on his ride to follow to the hospital. But when they were there, he... Texas didn't go inside. Dad said he could see how scared he was about the news, even knowing you were already breathing. Dad thinks he was worried something else would happen."

I could feel Swan's gaze on me, her hands on mine, but as I stared at the ground, all that was in my mind were her words and the pictures it conjured.

But then she continued softly, "Dad said Texas was in a state of anguish. Texas had gone to call Dodge, but Dad heard him choke on the words. He took the phone from Texas and told Dodge what happened. Maya, do you understand where I'm going with telling you this?"

It couldn't be true.

Not after all this time.

No. He still saw me as his friend's sister.

It couldn't. But....

"Maya?"

A shiver raked over my body, and I lifted my head to

meet her gaze with my watery one. "That I mean something to him."

"You do."

But what did I do with this information? Could I
actually allow it to sink in? What happened if I did and it
was wrong? I didn't know, but I couldn't stop thinking
about every single word and all the possibilities.

Later that night, I sat in an armchair in the corner of
my room, watching the TV mounted on the wall. I
wondered if Swan was still awake in her room, but then
again, she probably didn't have Texas on her mind. I
gripped the armrests on the chair, willing my brain to stop
ticking over with the knowledge of Texas liking me.

Texas.

A man I'd always been attracted to.

I ran my hands up and down the armrests and glanced
down at the left one, noticing I'd placed the clean towel
there. I bit my bottom lip when the sudden erotic thought
entered. My heart pounded behind my ribs. My pussy
clenched and belly tingled as my arousal spiked.

Scraping my top teeth over my bottom lip, I stood up.

Was I really going to do this?

The room suddenly heated more as I slipped my sleep
shorts down my legs. I kept my panties on when I straddled the armrest over the towel. With one foot on the floor
and the other on the cushion of the chair, I tightened my
thighs as I lifted my tee up to pull it over my head. I threw
it towards the bed before I glided my hands over my
breasts and rocked down over the chair.

A gasp escaped me. What would Texas think if he could see me now?

Resting one hand to the back of the chair, I pinched my nipple with the other and shifted forward more to press my clit into the fabric. Rocking back and forth, my hips stuttered a little when desire tingled through my groin and belly.

Would Texas like to watch as I got off?

Would he be turned on?

Would he touch himself?

"Oh God," I moaned from the thought of him watching and wanking. I slapped my other hand to the back of the chair, sliding my pussy back and forth over the hardness. It rubbed in the right place, and I could feel how wet it was making me. My panties would be drenched by the time I was done.

What would Texas do if I handed him my soaked underwear? Would he smell them? Taste them? Wish it was me he licked instead?

My back arched, my head dropped back, and I opened my mouth in a silent moan as my orgasm crashed through me. Panting, a laugh escaped me as I wondered what it actually would be like if I did have Texas with me. All I could think was that it'd be out of this world.

CHAPTER THIRTEEN

TEXAS

*T*alon had called for church. The only difference to this one was that we had to head to Caroline Springs for it to meet up with that charter there. I didn't mind at all. None of us did if it meant we got a ride out of it. It was easy to organise for the day off. I made sure my clients were pretty chill and understood that things like this could happen.

Talon rode at the front and centre, Griz and Blue just behind him, and then the rest were spread out. Coyote and I were someplace in the middle. Travelling with the brothers was always a goddamn thrill. It'd never get old, and always gave me a feeling of belonging.

This was family.

The weather was cool, but at least it wasn't raining.

All too soon, the time on the road flew by. It was nothing like the time since Maya had been away, which dragged, but at least she'd be home in just a few days.

Excitement rolled around in my gut.

Smiling to myself, I shook my head and knew I had to stop thinking about her to concentrate. We pulled into the compound's car park and stopped. Slipping off our rides, we were greeted by the brothers as we made our way into the building.

When Dodge entered the common room first, he turned to say to Talon, "We've cleared the compound out." On occasion, we all got together for church, and since there was a lot of us, we held it in the common room. Though, a lot of the time church was held separately, and then Dodge, like other presidents of different charters in Hawks, would report to Talon with anything that needed his attention. Honestly, I was glad today was the day we all met up, and damn grateful Talon had decided to take the trip to Melbourne for it instead of it being in Ballarat. It kept me occupied.

As soon as Talon sat at the head of the first table, the rest of us grabbed a seat where we could. I ended up at a table with Ruin, Coyote, Beast, Knife, and Cowboy.

Dodge sat on the other side of Talon, but I caught and returned his chin lift my way.

The room quieted as soon as Talon hit the gavel on the table. We talked about businesses and what was happening on the streets around both our territories, and that was when Dodge brought into the meeting intel about a new crew in town trying to push drugs and women. But it'd been noted that some of the women were turning up with bruises and cuts.

"The guys and I have it covered," Dodge said. "We're offerin' up help to the women where we can, but if they don't take it...."

There wasn't much else we could do.

Dodge then added, "Parker and Lan have the cops involved as well." Parker and Lan were detectives but had many contacts on the force who listened to them. "They're monitorin' them, gettin' enough evidence to take them down fully."

Talon grunted. "Good. And you know that if you need extra hands, the brothers and I from Ballarat aren't fuckin' far. Don't work everyone to the bone. Reach out. We're more than ready to help since things have settled in Ballarat."

Dodge nodded. "We will, and I'll keep you updated daily."

Talon nodded and moved onto other items that needed everyone's attention. All up, church lasted a couple of hours before he called it to an end.

Talon and Dodge stood, but it was Dodge who announced, "Time to fuckin' relax." He ordered some prospects to man the grill, and my gut growled at the thought of food.

Knife snorted. "Didn't eat this mornin'?"

Smirking, I rubbed my gut. "I did, but I'm still a growin' boy."

He snorted, and Beast shook his head.

Cowboy straightened. "Anyone want a drink?" Everyone gave him our orders, but Coyote went to help him.

"So, how's country livin' been for you?" Knife asked me, but then he caught Ruin glancing at his phone, which he'd been doing a lot. "You know you can be separate from your guy for a few fuckin' hours." He grinned teasingly.

Ruin rolled his eyes. "Says the guy who has his man right next to him all the time."

Knife glanced at Beast and back to Ruin. "We're not always together."

Beast chuckled, tagging the back of Knife's neck with his palm, shaking him a little before he dropped his hold and signed. *"He pouts if I'm not close."*

Knife sucked in a harsh breath and shoved Beast. "I do not, you fuckin' dick."

Everyone chuckled just as a seat was pulled back and Pick sat. His hard gaze stayed on me, and if I didn't know the guy, I would have been more intimidated by the look.

"What?" I clipped.

"My woman has it in her head that you're into her niece. If you are, I gotta see what your intentions are, brother, because Maya does not get fucked around."

Tensing, I ground my teeth together and glanced around us. "Keep your fuckin' voice down."

"Wait, it's true?" Knife asked.

Ruin said nothing, since he knew where I was at with

my feelings for Maya. But Beast looked just as surprised as his partner.

"Talon doesn't know?" Pick questioned.

"No. And seriously, until Maya knows anythin', it's not anyone's business. *Yet.* But since this is Maya, and she means the world to so fuckin' many, just know my intentions are nothin' but good. I'd never fuck her over, and that's all I'm gonna say on the matter."

Pick studied me for a beat before he slapped a hand to my back. "All right then. Don't stress—Josie will keep her lips shut. She ain't like a lot of the women."

I nodded and glanced around us again as he walked off. Fuckin' lucky no one else with a big damn mouth overheard or I'd have more people to deal with.

"You knew." Knife pointed a finger at Ruin.

"Duh" was all Ruin said.

Coyote and Cowboy handed out drinks and sat back down. "What'd we miss?" Cowboy asked.

The lot of us went silent.

Coyote and Cowboy stared at us. Until Coyote snorted. "Yeah, that's not suss at all. We talkin' about Texas and how he wants my sister as his old lady?"

Beast's and Knife's gazes widened.

Cowboy scoffed. "Oh, that."

Wait.

"What do you mean by *that*? You didn't know."

He huffed. "Please. If anyone saw you two in a room together lately, it's clear to see your interest. I read it clearly that day at the Harley store."

Well, fuck.

More laughs sounded around the table.

I didn't think my feelings were that obvious back then. But shit, maybe I have had stars and hearts in my eyes for a long time. Not that I cared Cowboy had figured it out or even Beast and Knife. They'd keep their mouths shut, though, because I was yet to convince Maya.

"You know you're gonna get hell from everyone, right?" Cowboy asked.

"Yep."

"And you're still gonna go for it?"

"In time... when I know she's ready, then yeah, I am. She's worth any shit I'll get."

Coyote gave me a nod. He knew I wouldn't fuck around with his sister.

"Aww," Ruin cooed while ruffling my hair.

I shoved his hand off. "Like you can talk."

To prove my point, his phone chimed, and he was all over it in seconds. "Don't care if everyone knows I'm smitten. Gotta call my boo."

"I think I just threw up in my mouth, hearing Ruin calling anyone boo," Coyote said.

"Fuck off," Ruin bit out, but his grin told us he didn't give a shit about the teasing. He left, taking his drink with him.

Knife hummed under his breath. "This explains why you moved. So, I'm guessin' you're lovin' country life?"

Grinning, I nodded.

Knife turned to Cowboy. "Looks like you'll be next."

Cowboy's cheeks shot to red, and he shrugged. "I'd be honoured to find my forever someone."

Cowboy, who was only twenty and not long out of being a prospect, had the biggest damn heart out there. Any woman or man would be treated like a queen or king by that guy. I looked forward to seeing him fall.

Damn, maybe falling for someone did make us mushy, but fuck if I cared.

CHAPTER FOURTEEN

TEXAS

*F*uck me, I was a jittery mess, knowing Maya was coming home. Hell, I'd even taken the day off. It was lucky I did, since I could barely concentrate. Not that I knew I'd be seeing her. It'd seem too weird if I dropped in on the day that I knew she got back, like some lovesick fool. And yeah, that was me admitting I was falling hard for this woman. My feelings had grown even more with the time we'd spent together or talked on the phone or in texts.

While I'd said it before, now I was more sure.

Maya Marcus was mine, and Christ, I wanted to goddamn pray she saw me as hers.

Had I gotten under her skin again?

Was she crushing on me again?

Did she think of me like I did her?

"No offense, but can you fuck off?" Dodge complained with a sigh.

I'd even gone for a ride to Melbourne so I wouldn't be waiting on Maya's doorstep when she pulled up. Okay, so Dodge found my pacing annoying since I was doing it alongside a car he was working on in the mechanics business connected to the Caroline Springs compound.

Stopping, I turned to glare while crossing my arms over my chest. "Sorry, is my pacing gettin' on your nerves?"

"That and you've been mumblin' to yourself for the last half an hour."

I snorted. I had not. "Bullshit."

"You have," Knife called. I shot him the finger.

"Someone's on his mind," Billy called, and I could hear the smile in his voice.

"Fuck off," I clipped.

Dodge's phone chimed. He pulled it out, read whatever was on it, and grinned before he announced, "The girls are home safe. We don't have to hunt anyone down."

My heart tripped over its beat.

Maya was back.

A few brothers chuckled. We all knew Talon had been worried, and not that Griz would admit it aloud, but he'd been just as concerned about his daughter as well.

I rocked on my feet, already wanting to head back to Ballarat to see her. But I didn't want to crowd her. She'd probably need to rest or something.

"Hey." Dodge stepped closer and dipped his head in. "Just go see her."

"Nah, I'm cool. She's home. That's good." I nodded to myself. I knew she'd enjoyed herself in Queensland but had also missed home. On the last night, when we'd talked over the phone, she'd told me she really did need the time away but still wasn't sure where she wanted her career to go. Hopefully, I'd reassured her enough by letting her know there wasn't a need to rush. That I was sure her bosses understood. Anyone would.

Dodge studied me and sighed. "Why you holdin' back?"

"Because I fucked up to start with by not seeing her. I don't want to rush this. The timin's gotta be perfect, and then I hope to Christ she'll agree to an us and seein' a future with me."

He reached out and ruffled my hair. "My wittle boy's growin' up."

I glared and smacked his hand away, but I couldn't hide the smirk. "Shut it, old man."

But in all honesty, during the last few months, even I felt like I'd finally grown up. Become the man I'd always wanted to be. A good man. With good people at my back. I had my own worth within my businesses. Now all I needed was the special woman at my side.

"You stayin' in town tonight then?" Dodge asked.

"Has Low made my room into a theatre yet?"

Dodge scoffed. "Like she'd ever do it. It's the same as you left it."

"Yeah, I reckon I'll stay." Then at least I didn't look too desperate to see Maya.

"Good. Now help me finish this to keep your mind busy."

My phone chimed, and I pulled it out of my back pocket.

MAYA:

> Want to come for dinner?

My gut gave off a nervous and yet excited jig.

She wanted to see *me*.

Me. After being away, and even though we'd talked every day, she wanted to see me.

Jesus, the hope in me flashed bright and made me damn giddy. "Actually, I've now got other plans." Grinning, I saluted Dodge. "Catch you soon."

Chuckling, he shook his head. "You're whipped, boy."

I snorted. "Just like you were and still are."

"Can't argue with that."

On my way out, I messaged back, asking what time I was needed.

MAYA:

> Seven.

That gave me enough time to get back to Ballarat.

ME:

See you then. Glad you made it home
safe.

The fact she'd wanted me to come to dinner, to see
me, and the smiley face emoji she'd sent back had me all
floaty and shit on the ride back to Ballarat.

When I pulled up out the front of Talon's place, I
climbed off my ride and looked down at myself. Shit, was I
supposed to change? Did jeans, long-sleeve top, and club
vest look okay when Maya had invited me to dinner? I'd
had dinner at their place before, but to me, this was something more. She wanted to see me on the day she got
home. It was dinner with the family, right?

Fuck.

I had to stop thinking; it didn't do me any favours.

Stalking up the walkway, I jumped the stairs onto the
front porch and knocked. The door swung open, and my
breath was knocked out of me.

Maya stood with one hand on the door, smiling
brightly up at me. "Hey, stranger."

"Fuck," I uttered before I swept down and scooped
her up into a tight hug. I buried my nose in her hair and
took a whiff like an addict. Jesus, she smelled good, and
damn had I missed it. "Maya," I whispered into her hair.

Her arms tightened around my neck. When I dropped
her back to her feet, she looked up at me with a strange
expression, but it was quickly replaced with a sweet smile.

I couldn't stop myself from bopping her on her cute
button nose. "Good to see your face."

"Good to be seen. I can't believe I missed this cold weather."

I snorted as she stepped back and I entered. "It's gonna get colder yet."

She groaned. "Don't remind me."

"How was your last day in the sunshine?"

"Loved it, but I'm glad to be home." She shut the door and started down the hall. "Everyone's already in the kitchen. You're a little early, so were just hanging around together, getting dinner ready and talking."

"Wicked."

My gaze slid to her arse as we made our way down the hall. Fuck, I wanted permission to touch it, spank it, even bite it. My cock throbbed behind my jeans. It wasn't the time for dirty thoughts when I had to sit at the table with her dad who was my president. Knowing Talon, he could probably pick up on shit like that.

I happened to run my eyes down to her hands at her side and noticed they were shaking slightly.

Was she okay?

Did she need to sleep?

Reaching out, I took her wrist in hand and pulled her to a stop. Maya turned towards me, a question written on her raised brows. I lifted her hand. "Are you okay?"

A blush hit her cheeks as she tugged her wrist free and laughed slightly. "Yeah, fine. Just tired." She reached up and patted my arm with a gentle look, then turned and entered the dining and kitchen area. "Texas is here," she called after I followed her through.

I couldn't help but think something was going on with Maya. There was a slight hesitation and shyness in her actions. Something I wasn't used to seeing from her. At least not recently.

What happened? Did I do something I didn't know about? Was the hug at the front door too much? Fuck, did she meet someone in Queensland?

I'd kill them.

Shaking my head, I greeted everyone, but I couldn't stop thinking that something had changed. Maya kept glancing at me and looking away.

"How's business?" Talon asked when I sat at the table. Zara, Maya, and the twins were in the kitchen, still preparing the meal, but Ruby had pushed me towards the table to take a seat.

"Good. Still can't believe how busy it's been since I opened."

"People are gonna look you and your work up. Your place in Melbourne's got a good rep."

A beer was placed in front of me. I tipped my head back and caught Maya's gentle grin. "Thanks, babe."

As soon as the words were out, I fucking froze. I was sure I hadn't called Maya "babe" in front of Talon. While he knew we were friends, he didn't have a clue I wanted his daughter as mine, right? Fuck, what if he knew? That was a whole conversation I hadn't been prepared for tonight.

When Maya went back to help her mum, I swallowed

thickly and slowly looked back at Talon. His jaw clenched, his hand tightening around his drink.

Fuck.

Did he read into the words? The look? Had I stared at his daughter too long?

The bastard was a smart man. A guy I looked up to in many ways. Like I did Dodge.

He wasn't stupid. Would he brush it off or say something?

Could I fix this before it blew up in my face and he started saying shit in front of Maya, who didn't even know how deep my feelings went for her?

Did I man up and take him out of the room to talk with him myself? Ask his blessing or whatever? Was it too soon, since I didn't even have a clue where Maya's head and heart were at about me?

Jesus fucking Christ, I was going to break my damn brain thinking this hard.

"Prez, can I have a word?" The words were out of my mouth before I could backtrack and second-guess myself.

I didn't know if his daughter would even be on board with something with me, but I wanted to show respect to Talon and let him know where my head was at.

Talon stood. When his chair scooted back on the floor, the noise caught the attention of everyone else.

"What's going on?" Maya asked.

"Nothin'. We just gotta talk about work," Talon said, his tone hard.

"Talon?" Zara called.

"It's fine, kitten. Won't be long."

Maya frowned, worry clear in her eyes when she looked at me. I tried for a reassuring smile, but I wasn't sure I pulled it off.

My heart damn trembled inside my chest. I wasn't scared of Talon, but he was Maya's father, and if he couldn't see me in his daughter's life, he could make my life hell. He could sway Maya against me.

Talon took me into his office. "Take a seat," he ordered and closed the door.

Shit, sweat licked the back of my neck and palms.

Suddenly, it felt like my life was on the line.

In a way, it was, because Maya *was* my life.

Talon walked around his desk to sit behind it. He rocked back on his chair and stared at me. I waited a beat to see if he would say anything. To see if he'd noticed my attraction to Maya was more than friendship. Would Maya be pissed I went to her father to share my feelings first? To get his permission to court his daughter like the old-fashioned way?

Christ, I felt screwed either way, and no matter what, I was going to mess up with someone.

Talon cleared his throat. "You're the one who wanted to talk, so talk."

"Did *you* need me to talk?"

His brow rose. "What do you think I would want you to talk about?"

I rubbed my sweaty palms down my thighs. Shit, I had to go with my gut. He was the President of Hawks, but he also meant a lot more than that, and he was Maya's father.

But before I could open my mouth, he demanded, "Tell me the real reason you moved to Ballarat."

And there it was. He knew. He'd always known, and yet he'd accepted me in Ballarat, into his club.

"Because there was someone I wanted to get close to."

He gripped his armrests. "My daughter that someone?"

"Yes, Prez."

"You think I'm fuckin' stupid, brother?"

"No."

He leaned forward, resting his arms on his desk. "I reckon you do."

"I don't."

"I know when I see a man lose his shit over his woman bein' hurt"—I stilled as he continued—"that the man is a good one. One who cares a great fuckin' deal for his woman. One who'll protect her, do anythin' for her. Back her in anythin' she picks to do."

I ground my teeth together to try and stop the onslaught of emotions coursing through me.

"It goddamn kills me to see my kids grow up, brother. One day you'll understand it. One day when you've got your old lady at your side and a brood of your own, you'll get the torment a father goes through."

Hope fucking lit inside of me.

"At least I'll know Maya's in good hands, and, Texas, *if* she accepts you, I know she'll have a good life with a hardworkin' man who knows he'd have his arse handed to him if he fucks over my daughter in any way."

The threat didn't surprise me. I'd expected it. Being protective was in his blood. Having heard his blessing, though.... Fuck, I didn't fully understand how much it would mean. It was like a weight had been lifted off me even as the emotions from it all held my chest in a tight clamp.

Clenching my jaw, I closed my eyes and nodded. Opening them after a beat, I cleared my throat. "She'll be treasured each and every fuckin' day."

Talon held my gaze and grunted. "*If* she accepts you."

Nodding again, I agreed by saying, "If."

And if I could ask for luck, I would when it came to having Maya accept me as her man.

CHAPTER FIFTEEN

MAYA

"*W*hat do you think that was about?" I whispered to Mum after she sprinkled the chicken with cheese and slipped the dish back into the oven. Ruby and Drake were arguing about something as they made the salad.

Mum leaned against the counter. "I'm not completely sure."

Tearing my eyes away from the hallway, I faced her. "But you have an idea?"

She sighed. "Sweetie, we all heard Texas call you 'babe.'"

I threw out a hand. "So? He's always called me something."

Drake groaned and turned to us. "Tell me you're not

that dense? Anyone can see what's right in front of you. Shit, Texas is here all the time, and it's not to see Dad. Them talkin' was bound to happen."

"Drake, don't be an ass about it," Ruby snapped.

Staring at the floor, I gripped the counter behind me, my knees suddenly feeling weak. Drake was right. I was being dense. I'd even managed to push Swan's words to the back of my mind. Every time they tried to pop back up, I forced myself to think of something else.

I had to. If I didn't, I'd be a nervous wreck, knowing there was a high chance Texas *liked* me.

Somehow, I'd managed to text normally after what Swan had said. I'd wanted to make sure to keep our new friendship in case she was wrong. It was why I invited him over after getting back. Besides the fact that I missed him, I needed to figure out how to act around him. If I hadn't organised to see him straight away, my overthinking would have made everything too awkward.

But then he'd gone and hugged me. And not just any friendly hug. The hug was tight and strong, possessive... as if I'd been gone for a year and not two weeks. If it hadn't been for the way I'd lost my ability to think, I would have been calmer. I wouldn't have thought of Swan's words. I wouldn't have let hope blossom.

"Swan—" I cleared my throat. "—told me what her dad saw that night when I.... She told me how Texas acted," I said softly to the floor.

Mum took my hand in hers, and I looked into her heartfelt gaze. "I saw him at the hospital, sweetheart.

You've guarded your heart for so long against him, knowing he was blind to you. *Now* he sees you. His eyes are wide open, and now it's up to you if you want to take the chance on him."

My already racing pulse kicked up to another speed.

"I... I...." I wanted to dive headfirst into something with Texas. I did. But I couldn't ignore the doubt whispering through my mind.

He doesn't really want you.

He's just being nice.

People are reading into something that's not there.

He'll see someone else and drop you.

He's not looking for his forever.

He'll break your heart.

Mum squeezed my hand. "You don't have to make a decision now. There's no need to rush."

Nodding, I released Mum's hand and went to the refrigerator. "Um, do you want the dressings out for the salad?"

"Sure, sweetie."

I heard Ruby and Drake muttering back and forth. I was worried Drake would say something in front of Texas, but I knew Ruby would have my back. Honestly, I feared for my own reactions when Texas returned, but more than that, I wondered what they were talking about in that room.

Was it really about work or was it something else?

Could it really be because Texas had called me "babe" in front of Dad? I was sure Texas had used endearments on me before in front of him. I was used to hearing "baby" or "babe" from Texas, so I didn't take notice of who he said it in front of.

Then again, why would Dad care? He'd used "babe" or "darlin'" for other women. They really didn't mean anything. Not that I needed to worry about this. It wasn't like Texas was in there confessing his feelings for me to my father.

That was, if he had

All right, I was 80 percent sure Texas liked me. The clues kept piling up.

But dear God, the thought of it, of knowing, drove my mind and body into a tailspin.

I didn't know if I wanted to vomit or sit on the toilet for the next half hour, crapping myself, since my body was in that much of a state.

Texas was into me.

After all these years.

After placing the condiments on the table, I pressed my hand against my twisting belly.

I really loved getting to know him these past few weeks. I also regretted getting my feelings involved when we were young. If I hadn't crushed on him, we could have been good friends back then too.

What happened if I took the chance now but it ruined our friendship?

God, even the thought of diving in caused havoc to my system. I wanted to laugh, to scream, to cry, to smile so wide there was a risk my face would crack. I was over-the-moon happy, yet scared, and also surprised at the fact I was turned on, and worried, and turned on some more.

Okay, it was good to say the thought of being able to kiss, to hold, and even be intimate with Texas was wild.

If I started something with him, I would get to touch him. I would get to run my hands over his smooth, inked skin. Curl my fingers in his trimmed beard and get to tug his head down so I could finally kiss his sweet lips again.

Would he taste the same?

Could the kiss be more than what I remembered? It had been blow-my-socks-off amazing when I'd been sixteen. What would be blown off this time?

If it happened.

If I took the chance.

Groaning inwardly, I went back to grab the salad bowl and placed it on the table.

I was getting ahead of myself. I didn't completely know Texas wanted more with me. But then, if he did, when would he make a move? Then again, if he made a move, was I ready to jump?

My heart skipped a beat when I heard Dad's office door open and their pounding footsteps come down the hall shortly after. When they entered, I froze on the spot, standing beside the table. I listened to them laugh about something, but didn't hear what the words were.

At least they were chuckling. That was good, right? Then again, I didn't really know what they'd been talking about in the office.

When Texas glanced my way, I stupidly lifted my hand and pointed to the counter and yelled, "Dinner."

The room quieted, except for Drake's snickering. I winced, blushed, and rushed to the counter.

"What the...?" sounded from Dad.

"Honey, come place the dish on the placemats on the table for me," Mum said. "Texas, take a seat. Do you need another beer?"

"I'm good, thanks."

"Okey-dokey. Ruby and Drake, grab the rest of the things and let's eat."

Everyone moved while I stood, holding up the counter, or it held up me. That was until I felt heat at my back.

"All right, Maya?" Texas's quiet tone caressed my ear as he placed a hand on my hip.

In a panic, I picked up the spatula and swung it around, nearly clocking him in the head. Thankfully, he grabbed my wrist in time.

"Yep." I nodded. "Just needed this. Sorry. Let's go eat."

Drake snorted, and I heard a slight slap, then my brother mumbled under his breath. My wrist dislodged from Texas's grip, I moved over to the table and took a seat next to the one Texas had vacated. Drake sat on my other side. I didn't pick the spot to begin with, but I had to leave seats open on the other side for—

"We're here," Cody yelled from the front of the house.

Leaning into Texas a little, I ignored the flutter and

pushed the nerves aside to try and act normal as I whispered, "We better get some food before he gets to the table, or it'll all be gone."

Texas grinned down at me, and my breath caught.

A hand settled on my neck. "Too right, sister."

"Hi, everyone," Channa greeted, and we all replied as she moved around the table to sit next to Ruby. My gaze widened slightly when I took in her crazy hair and what looked like a fresh mark on her neck. Cody, after he kissed Mum on the cheek, took the only spare chair left on Channa's other side, which was also next to Dad who was at the head of the table. Mum sat at the other end.

"Looks and smells amazing, Zara," Channa commented before she added, "Sorry we're late. I had to take the dogs for a walk and then we ran into an old neighbour."

Was that a leaf in her hair?

Discreetly and while the others chatted, I tugged on my own hair and gave Channa wide eyes. She didn't catch on right away. Even looked at me as if I'd lost my mind until I mouthed, "Hair."

She quickly fixed her hair, and heat hit her cheeks when the leaf fluttered to the table. "Thank you," she mouthed.

"I'm thinkin' of gettin' some ink," Cody told Texas.

"What would you get?" Mum asked.

"Not sure yet, but I wanna cover an arm."

"Sure you can hack the pain?" Dad teased with a smirk.

"If you can do it, Dad, so can I."

I glanced down at my plate just as I picked up the tongs for some chicken but noticed my plate already had food on it. I paused for a beat, dropped the tongs, and glanced at Drake. He tipped his chin towards Texas and I looked there, but he was busy telling Cody to drop by his shop.

He'd filled my plate.

He'd served me like Cody did Channa. Like Dad would Mum, if they sat closer.

My belly fluttered.

"You should drop by one time too, Maya."

It was another clue he liked me, right?

Another clue that he wanted me in his life as more than a friend, right?

None of my other male friends served up my meal.

"*Maya's* off with the fairies tonight," Mum said.

"Sorry?" I called.

Cody snorted. "Too much sun in Queensland." Cody, like my whole family, had checked in with me every now and then while I'd been away.

I nodded. "That's got to be it." But what had I missed?

"I asked if you wanted to drop by the shop one time?"

Swallowing thickly, I nodded. "Yeah. Yep. Sure. Sounds good." I'd get to see where Texas worked all his magic. I could even make it a time when he was working so I could see him in action.

"How was Queensland?" Cody asked. I drew my eyes to his concerned ones.

I was acting like a wanker. I needed to get myself under control and push all romantic thoughts of Texas to the back of my mind.

"You already know how it was by calling me all the time."

"It was lucky I did that one time or that guy—"

"What guy?" Texas blurted.

All eyes went to him, and I didn't miss Cody's satisfied smirk.

Texas stared down at me. "There was a guy?"

"No. Cody's being an idiot."

Texas faced Cody. "What guy?"

"Just a douche at the coffee house Maya had been in."

"Yes, and tell everyone what you yelled through the phone, please." I sat back and glared.

Cody started chuckling. "I yelled that her gonorrhoea test results came back positive."

The table erupted into laughter. Dad even reached over and patted Cody's arm.

Texas turned to me and dipped his chin down while they talked about it. "Were you gonna go out with him?"

I jerked my head back in shock, eyes wide. "What? No. Not at all."

He studied my face and then nodded before he went back to eating, contributing to the conversation when needed.

If my stomach wasn't in such a state, I would have

eaten more, but I couldn't. I also skipped on dessert. Still, I enjoyed the night. It was always good to sit down with the whole family for a good meal. Even more so when Texas was beside me.

Goddamn, I was treading in thick water, and the surface led me to Texas each and every time.

Especially when he grinned at me like he was doing as we stood in the doorway while we said goodbye to everyone who had to leave.

"Hey, Maya, Texas. Cody and I are going to check out a band early tomorrow night at a local pub. Do you guys want to join us?"

"Oh, um...."

"I've got nothin' on. Sounds good," Texas said. He knocked his hip against mine. "You'll come?"

Smiling, I nodded. "Sure." Back to Channa, I said, "Thanks for the invite."

"No problem. Thanks again for dinner, Zara," she called.

"You're welcome, sweetheart. Drive safe, Cody."

"Will do, Mum."

"Later," Texas called with a salute, his gaze on me for an extra beat before he spun and walked away. I closed the door, turned, and leaned against it. Dad had already disappeared, but there stood Drake, Ruby, and Mum.

"You were really smooth, sis. Didn't act *any* different," Drake said.

"Really?" I asked, brows high.

He snorted. "No." He chuckled, shaking his head as he walked off. "Night, all."

We all called back good nights, mine a little grumblier than Mum's and Ruby's.

Ruby smiled brightly. "This is going to be epic. I can't wait until you two get together."

"I'm not sure that'll happen." There went that hope again, doing somersaults in my belly.

Ruby laughed, and even Mum cackled as she stepped close and kissed my cheek. "Get some rest. It's good to have you home."

"Thanks, Mum." It was good to be home. Though, when it came to Texas, I wasn't sure my heart or head could take what could happen if we continued to dance around this unspeakable thing between us.

CHAPTER SIXTEEN

TEXAS

*M*aya bounced her knee where she sat in the passenger seat of my car. She'd acted different last night, and it seemed like it was going to happen again. What was going on? Why did she suddenly seem nervous around me?

She rubbed her hands down her thighs and took a shaky breath.

"Babe."

She glanced at me and then away. "Uh, yeah?"

"What's goin' on?"

She huffed. "What? Nothing. What's going on with you?"

Drawing my brows down in confusion, I pulled to a stop at the red light and turned to her. "Maya, you're bein' all jittery." I pointed down at her knee, which promptly stopped.

She bit her bottom lip and ran her hand over the side of her neck. "I-I guess it's... ah...." She scrunched up her nose. Was she trying to think of something to say? "Easton called today. He mentioned that he, Lan, and Parker were hoping to come to the pub tonight for the band. But... I mean, I could tell he wanted to bring up work on the phone, but he didn't. I'm just not sure if he will or won't tonight if I see him."

I get that she'd be apprehensive talking about it, but I didn't think it'd make her this nervous.

Reaching over, I placed a palm on her thigh, just above her knee, and squeezed before putting both hands back on the steering wheel when the light turned green. "Don't stress about it. Give me a code word if you want out of a conversation, and I'll get you out."

I could feel her gaze on me, but I didn't look her way to catch it.

"Thanks. I guess I could say 'Pepsi.'"

"Pepsi?"

"Yes."

"Okay, Pepsi it is." I grinned, thinking she was cute. "You heard anythin' about this band?"

"No. But I did look them up, and they sound good."

"At least there's that."

"Thanks again for offering to pick me up."

"It's on the way. Thought it'd be sensible." Shit, did

that sound like I was doing it just because and not me wanting that extra time with her alone?

She hummed. "True."

Fuck. Did her tone sound off? Had she taken it the wrong way? Was she ready for the right way though? The truth?

Before I could correct anything, or actually think of the right thing to say—I also thought it best to leave it in case I fucked it up—I pulled into a car park down the road from the pub. The street was busy, but not too much. Christ, I hoped it wasn't too crowded. Crowds annoyed me. It also meant there was a chance some guys would take notice of Maya.

Who was I kidding? Of course she'd be noticed by other guys. She was stunning. I glanced down at her jeans when we met at the front of my car. I'd already noticed how they hugged her arse nicely. There were a little too many cuts and slits for others to look at, though. The shirt she had on was cut low enough for a taste of cleavage but wasn't over-the-top bare all. Thank fuck.

Placing a hand on her lower back, I led her down the footpath. She glanced up at me with a small smile that had my gut damn well fluttering.

Christ, she was beautiful. I wanted to thread my fingers into her long, dark-brown hair. It was so damn thick and wavy. But I refrained. Hopefully one day.

The closer we got, the louder the noise spilled from the bar. Coyote and Channa were already inside. Coyote had texted, letting me know they'd grabbed a booth on the far side. We just had to get in there and find it.

Maya took out her purse to pay the fee to get in, but I'd already had the money in my pocket and handed it over top of her.

She looked over her shoulder with a glare. "You didn't have to."

I winked. "I know."

She grumbled something under her breath that I couldn't hear as we walked down the hall. When it opened up to the main area, I took in the room quickly, noting all the exits as a just in case. I also spotted Coyote and Channa. Leaning down, I said into Maya's ear, "Over to the right."

With my hand still on her back, I caught her shiver. That meant she was reacting to me, right? Was it my touch? Or talking close to her ear?

Shit, had my breath stunk and she shivered in revulsion?

I wasn't sure if I was supposed to remove my hand or not now. How did I become so indecisive when it came to a woman?

Usually, I'd know what to do. I'd know what women wanted. But I was second-guessing myself with everything when it came to Maya.

Coyote and Channa stood, since his woman was shoving at him to get out of their side of the booth. Channa wrapped her arms around Maya and hugged her close. The beaming smile on Maya's lips lit up her entire face. I was sure even her damn eyes glowed.

Fuck me.

I did know why I was scared I'd mess up. It was because she meant a fuckload more than any of the women in my past.

Maya was my future. The woman who'd stand at my side for the rest of our lives.

So yeah, I'd worry over shit because she was the most important person in my life.

Not that she knew it yet.

Thinking about telling her had my gut in a tight grip of nerves.

Coyote shook my hand, and we hugged one armed. "Your girl tanked?" I asked when I shifted back to see Channa gripping Maya's shoulders and shaking her a little while she talked a mile a minute.

Coyote chuckled. "Yeah, a little." He watched her like *she* was *his* forever. Though, I could have called it from the start. Even though I'd done a little harmless flirting with Channa to begin with, it'd been all in fun and so I could see Coyote get riled by it. Which was proof enough that subconsciously he'd known she was his also.

She was good for him and he for her.

Only, she was also shaking Maya a little too much for my liking. Chuckling, I stepped close and pulled Maya back against my chest. "You'll rattle her brain."

Channa straightened and grinned up at me. Coyote managed to curl his arm around her shoulders before she gave me two thumbs up and then raised her hands in the air. "Shots."

Maya laughed. "I'll start with a vodka first." I wasn't sure if she even realised that she'd rested against my chest more.

Channa spun to her man. "Cody, honey, let's get drinks."

Coyote smirked. "How about you take a seat, and I'll grab some drinks?"

"I'll help," I said.

The band's song changed. Channa gasped. "I love this song." She moved fast, grabbed Maya's hand, and dragged her out onto the dance floor.

"How many drinks has she had in the hour you've been here?"

"Two."

I jerked my head back in shock and looked at him. "Two?"

Chuckling, he nodded. "She's a bit of a lightweight."

Shaking my head, I glanced back to the women in time to see a couple of guys approaching them.

Fuck.

Coyote and I started forward. When we reached them, Coyote quickly stepped around the guy close to Channa and wrapped his arms around his woman's waist, pulling her tightly to him.

I tapped the other guy on his shoulder, and when he turned, I shook my head. "Don't even fuckin' think about it."

The sneer on his face told me he was going to press the matter, meaning my woman, but then his gaze flicked down to the vest I wore.

His hands rose in front of him. "No trouble. Didn't know she was yours."

Crossing my arms over my chest, I nodded. "Now you do."

The guys fled just before Maya looked over her shoulder. I grinned down and she moved close. "Enjoyin' them?"

"Actually, yeah. They sound better in person."

Nodding, I tapped her nose, and she smiled before turning back to the band.

I wanted to put my hands on her waist and pull her against me like she was already mine and I could lean down and kiss her neck, her cheek, and her lips. I clenched my hands at my sides as my heart went crazy in my chest at the thought of doing those things.

I'd give my left nut for Maya to turn around and kiss me.

Actually, I'd give both my nuts for Maya to turn and tell me her feelings had never changed. That she still wanted me.

Unfortunately—well, not really unfortunate, since I wanted to keep both my balls—that didn't happen.

Instead, I dipped down close to her ear and said, "Gonna get drinks. Stick close to your brother."

She turned her head enough to catch my gaze, and she nodded.

I ran my eyes over her face and noticed how close we were.

Could I lean in and kiss her?

Would she want me to?

Was it too soon?

Fuck. I didn't know, and until I got a clear signal from her, I wouldn't risk it. Not yet.

Straightening, I caught Coyote's attention and jerked my chin towards the front. "I'll grab drinks. You stay here."

"You got it, brother," he called.

As I made my way to the bar, I kept glancing back in case Coyote's attention was only on his woman, leaving Maya unprotected. He was lucky, it wasn't. At the bar, I took a stool and waited my turn while watching Maya sway her hips side to side.

There went the fluttering in my gut again.

Fluttering.

I'd never had that reaction before or even thought of that word.

In the past, my dick got hard over women, but the rest of my body hardly reacted. That was until Maya had opened my eyes.

Smirking, I shook my head at my own thoughts.

Glancing back down the other end of the bar, I glared at the two bartenders talking with, no doubt, some of their mates and ignoring the rest of us. I rested my elbows on the bar and leaned down for the wait.

A sigh sounded beside me on the right. I glanced there

to see a redheaded woman before looking over my shoulder to the dance floor. With a smirk, Coyote still watched both of them while they danced.

"Do you think they'll ever get down here?"

Shit. The woman was trying to talk to me. I was sure of it.

Wanting to get out of there quickly and back to Maya, I put a couple of fingers between my lips and whistled. The bartenders looked our way, and I waved them over.

"Thank God," the woman said. "Thanks."

With a chuckle, I told her, "Just thirsty." I seriously hadn't done it for her.

"My name's Holly. What's yours?"

"Texas."

"What can I get you?" one of the bartenders asked me while the other served Holly.

I ordered two beers for Coyote and me, a vodka and raspberry for Maya, and then I was stuck on Channa. I didn't have a clue what she drank. In the end, I grabbed another of Maya's drink. If she didn't like it, Maya could have it and I'd get Channa something else.

"So, Texas," Holly said, and I glanced back at her before she continued, "you here with others?"

"Yeah."

She smiled coyly. "A girlfriend?"

A hand touched down on my shoulder, and then a body pressed against my side. "I thought I'd come and help," Maya said from my left.

My dick jerked at her clear claiming actions. Hell, I couldn't be happier with it.

Turning my head, I grinned. "Thanks, babe." I straightened from leaning on the bar and curled an arm around Maya's shoulders. My lips twitched when I caught her staring at the woman on my other side.

Maya tipped her head back and whispered, "Am I interrupting?"

"Not at all." The bartender arrived with the drinks, I paid, and we took them back to the booth where Coyote and Channa were making out.

They only stopped when Maya slid into the other side of the booth. I took one of the glasses she'd been holding and put it in front of Channa. "Weren't sure what you drank so I got you one like Maya's."

Channa waved a hand around. "Thanks. I'll drink just about anything but wine."

I took the spot next to Maya and couldn't help myself; I shifted close enough to press my thigh against hers. I was still half hard from her actions earlier, and my gut wouldn't stop its dance. But I needed her close the hope she'd just given me meant a great fucking deal.

We chatted for a while. Channa complained about Stanley, an old guy who worked at her bakery, but it was only because he gave her shit in a loving way. Coyote told me he was getting in new gear at his Harley store, which I wouldn't mind checking out.

When I was done with my beer, I leaned back in the

booth and placed my arm along the cushion behind Maya, close to touching her shoulders.

When she was mine, I wouldn't have to stop myself from the casual touches I wanted to give her now. Grinning, I watched her every move as she told us a story about Drake. How she spoke with her hands, how animated she got, how her eyes lit. Hell, I could stare at her day and night if it wasn't creepy. She was damn mesmerising.

Christ, I wished she was mine now. The need to kiss her, taste her was strong. My body ached from it.

Soon.

If she kept showing me signs, I'd step up my game to make her mine and me hers.

When the conversation lulled, I leaned into her. "Guess Easton couldn't make it after all."

I made sure to watch her reaction. There was no missing her gaze flaring, her brows shooting up, the way she opened and closed her mouth. Only to open it to lie, "Ah, yeah... I guess not."

Why had she lied to me about him coming?

The only reason I could think of was that she'd been nervous about something else. Was it being around me with no one as a buffer? I'd thought we'd past that stage where she didn't want to be around me.

Unless her feelings had grown.

Unless she was into me.

That had to be it, right?

She'd always got out of my way when I was around because she liked me and was shy about it. A shyness that grew into annoyance when I kept bringing women around.

Only nowadays, that annoyance didn't rise; there'd be no one else I'd bring around since Maya was it for me.

Fuck yes.

"Why are you grinning like that?" Maya suddenly asked.

I pinched her chin and bopped her nose. "No reason."

Her gaze narrowed. "Yes, there is."

Winking, I tipped my chin towards her glass. "Want another?"

"Texas—"

I shifted into her space. "Tell you another time, yeah?"

A blush coated her cheeks, and I heard the slight intake of breath. "O-Okay," she whispered.

Yeah, I wasn't just being cocky. She was back being into me and knowing it had my body humming in elation. It was only a matter of days, or a day, or a couple of hours.... No, I'd stick with a couple of days to be completely sure Maya wanted me in the way I wanted her, and then I'd make my move.

Christ, my heart, soul, *and* dick were all for the next level.

CHAPTER SEVENTEEN

MAYA

*I*t was a few days after we'd seen the band, and I still couldn't get Texas off my mind. No longer were my thoughts based on friendship. That night at the pub, *I* had wanted to kiss him, and when I'd seen that woman looking at him like he was a juicy piece of meat, I couldn't stop myself from ending it.

He wasn't for her.

Though, at the time, and for a slight moment, I'd regretted my decision, so I'd asked Texas if I'd been interrupting. When he'd told me no, smugness rolled through me, and I'd wanted to hug him, kiss him, show her that he wasn't interested in anyone but me.

The only downside to the night was that I was positive Texas knew I'd lied about Easton wanting to come to see the band and how I'd been worried. But I'd panicked in the car, and that had been the first thing that popped into my mind, since earlier that day, I had actually chatted to Easton over the phone.

The truth was something I couldn't let Texas know, too nervous knowing he had feelings for me. Now, it was as if I no longer knew how to act around him when we were alone.

It didn't help that my own heart had started to cling to him again.

We spoke every day.

Sometimes more than once.

Those emotions for Texas I'd buried long ago had surfaced, and I was close to drowning in them. Now I wanted... *things*, intimate *things*, and I couldn't stop picturing them. What also didn't help was when we'd been alone in the car that night.

Scrubbing a hand over my face, I groaned and made my way into the kitchen.

"What are you moaning about?" Mum asked. "Also, I've just made a pot of coffee if you want one."

"I'm good, thanks, and nothing's wrong."

Her brows rose as she took a sip.

"Seriously, I'm fine." My steps faltered when it dawned on me. I *was* doing better. That night and John's death would always be in the back of my mind, but for once—and I wasn't sure how long it had been this way—the reminder of everything hadn't been at the forefront.

I wasn't sure if I liked that.

Guilt started to creep in.

"Maya?"

"Shouldn't I still be crippled from what happened? Losing John was gut-wrenching. How could I actually be happy?"

"Sweetie," Mum whispered. She put her mug down and came to me, sliding her hands down my arms. "Do you think I should live in the past and remember everything that's happened to the family?"

Tears formed in my eyes, but I shook my head.

"There is nothing wrong in finding happiness again. That pain will always live inside you, and you'll carry it for the rest of your life, but it's okay to keep living. To laugh, to smile, and love. You can't tell me John wouldn't want that for you."

"Your momma's right, child."

With a startled jump, I spun around to see Dad and Moreen standing just inside the kitchen.

The tears fell. "Moreen."

"Hush, sweet girl," she ordered, and made her way over to where she took both my hands in hers. "Do you think my John would want me to pine for him for months or even years?"

"No," I uttered.

"That's right. We've had many, many sad days, Maya. But it's been a couple of months since it happened. We learn to live with that sadness in the back of our minds and hearts. John would want us both to live life. Don't you go feeling guilty, you hear me?"

LILA ROSE

"Yes, Moreen."

"Good." She let go of my hands and went over to the counter to tap it. "Now, your momma promised me some cake, and I'm not seeing it yet."

Smiling softly, I glanced at Mum, who wiped at her eyes and let out a laugh. "It's in the fridge. The others should be here shortly."

"What's going on?" I asked.

"Just a get-together."

Dad snorted. "A gossip session. That means I'm outta here."

"Honey, you don't need to rush off," Mum said.

He went to her and gave her a kiss that had Moreen catcalling. Dad pulled back with a smirk. "I'm headin' to the compound."

"All righty," Mum said softly, staring in a daze up at him. Dad's smirk grew into a grin. She blinked and watched him leave after he said a quick goodbye to Moreen and me. Her gaze then turned to me. "Sweetie, I would have told you, but I thought you'd be busy with Texas."

"Texas? Who's this boy?" Moreen asked.

I scoffed, answering Mum, "It's not like we see each other all the time."

Mum told Moreen, "Texas is a member of Hawks. Just a bit older than Maya. They're friends."

"With benefits?"

I choked on my saliva. "Moreen, no."

She studied me. "But you want it to be."

That didn't sound like a question.

"I do not," I stated.

She rolled her eyes. "Child, it's as clear as day you're into this guy."

Sighing, I dropped my head back, eyes on the ceiling. When I looked back at her, I asked, "How is it so damn obvious?" Did Texas know? If he did, why hadn't he made a move?

"Just talking about him, your eyes get this soft look, and you get red in the cheeks. This is good, girl. John used to always say how he'd worry you weren't spending enough time socialising to meet someone. He worried you wouldn't find a love that burns bright like ours does." Her eyes glistened. "Now he's looking down, and I know he's not worried about you anymore."

"Moreen," I whispered.

"Come hug me and go see your beau."

"He's not my beau."

"Yet," Mum added.

"I.... Okay, maybe yet."

They both beamed.

"Come here, girl." Moreen opened her arms. I walked over and into them and they wrapped around me, like mine did her. "Be happy."

"I will."

"Good. Now go to your beau. I'm sure he can put a bigger smile on your face."

Mum giggled off to the side.

"I can't go see him. We're not dating, and it's not like he's asked me over."

"Pish-posh. You don't need an invite. If the boy's into you, he'll be thrilled to see you rock up without an invite."

"He's into her," Mum supplied. "Big time."

"Mum," I cried with a groan.

"What? He is."

"Yes, but knowing it freaks me out, and I'll just get nervous."

Moreen nodded. "That's good. Tells me he means a lot to you. I'm sure he feels the same way."

I scoffed. "He's always cool, calm, and collected."

"Whatever he is, I'm sure he'd love a drop-by from you," Moreen said again.

Thinning my lips, I glanced to the side and scratched my cheek. Could she be right? Would Texas like me to just stop by? "I don't know. He could still be working."

"What's he do?" Moreen asked.

"He's a tattooist."

"Ooh-wee, he already sounds hot. You got a photo to show me?"

I did. Texas and I sometimes sent photos in Snapchat, and I may have had them saved.

Taking out my phone, I unlocked it and brought one up before I turned the screen her way.

"Oh Lord." She clutched at her chest. "He is so hot, it's a sin." She snatched the phone from my hand and brought it closer to her face. "Those tats, that body, those eyes, that mouth, that goatee and 'stash. Even the bling he wears suits him. You snap him up, Maya Marcus."

Laughing, I shrugged. "I'll see."

Moreen snorted and met Mum's gaze. "Tell your girl to get out of here."

"Sweetie, do you want to see Texas?"

"Texas—did I mention his name is fine as well?" Moreen asked.

Smiling, I shook my head. But did I want to see him? "Yes, I do."

"Then take a chance and go drop by his place. If he's working, say you'll come back another time."

Straightening, I ran my hands down my tee and nodded. "Okay, I'm doing it." I nodded again.

"It's like she's getting ready for a big event," Moreen said.

"I am," I told her. "This is big—me dropping by his place." Well, to me it was. At least, I thought it was, because it showed him I wanted his time. Didn't it?

Oh God, I was going to be sick.

"Stop overthinking things, girl. Just do it."

"Right. Okay. I will."

A knock rattled the front door before it opened, and Deanna yelled, "Party, bitches."

Footsteps sounded down the hallway, and then Deanna, Ivy, Malinda, and Clary entered the room.

"What's going on?" Malinda asked.

"Just girl talk," Mum quickly said before Moreen could.

"I'm heading out. Have a good afternoon," I said with a smile.

"Where are you going?" Deanna asked.

"Out and about." I went to walk by her, but she grabbed my wrist.

"I was there when you were brought into the world. I know when something's going on. Tell Aunty Deanna all about it."

"Really, it's nothing. I'm just going to see a friend."

Her face brightened. "Texas?"

The others who had been greeting Mum and Moreen stopped talking and turned to us.

"Uh, yeah, well, we are friends."

"With benefits?" Ivy asked. "Not that you need to tell us. Really, we should mind our own business and know Maya will come to any of us if she wants to talk. But just so you know, Maya, we are here, any of us, if you need to chat about boy problems. God only knows we've had our fair share. I mean, have you seen our men?" She cackled. "Of course you have. But—"

"Dear Lord, get this woman a drink," Moreen put in.

The others laughed.

Ivy smiled. "I tend to ramble in awkward situations." She met my gaze. "I didn't want you to feel pressured, like you have to tell us anything."

"I know, and thank you. I am going to see Texas, and for now, we are *only* friends."

"For now?" Clary said.

"Yes. I think. I don't know. It's all scary."

"Ha," Malinda blurted. "We know that feeling. Just go with it."

Smiling, I nodded. "I will. Okay, I'm off."

"She's not moving," Moreen pointed out.

Deanna spun me around and shoved me towards the hall. "Get."

"Thanks," I called back, and made my way outside with my heart in my throat.

Why did I seriously feel this was a big step towards something huge?

CHAPTER EIGHTEEN

TEXAS

J had my head bent over my client's thigh, working on the scary-ass clown tattoo he wanted, when there was a knock on the door.

"Yeah," I called as I sat back and wiped over my work. I looked up when the door opened, and Mon stood there with a cheeky smile.

She leaned against the frame. "Someone's popped in to see you."

Those words with that smile had me suspicious. "Who?"

"A woman."

"Did you get a name?"

"Yep," Mon answered by popping the *p*.

Chris, my client, chuckled. He knew, like I did, that

Mon was being difficult.

"Mon," I warned.

"She's cute."

Rolling my eyes, I told her, "You want to stay employed, you'll give me a name now."

Was it Maya?

Could it be Maya?

She'd never come by before.

Would she now?

If it was her, why?

Shit. Fuck. Christ.

My heart was currently running its own race, as if it wanted to get out of my body and out the front to check for me.

"Her name's Maya."

"Maya's here?" I asked softly and with damn awe in my tone. My gut spun on a twirl.

She'd come to see me.

Mon gasped. "She's the one who's had you smiling lately."

"Now, this chick, I've got to meet," Chris said.

"Not like I've been a moody arsehole before now."

They both stared at me.

"Get lost, you two. Mon, tell Maya to come on back."

"You got it." She grinned.

I glanced down at Chris and saw his shit-eating smirk. "What?" I snapped.

"You're nervous. Damn, man, she is special."

"Not a fuckin' bad word to her," I warned. Chris was

a regular client, one who travelled from Melbourne to get my ink, and we'd known each other a while.

He gave me a salute. "Best behaviour."

I heard Mon talking rapidly about the place as they approached. I shifted in my seat, glanced down at my clothes and then back up. Chris started chuckling.

"Eat shit and die," I clipped.

His laughter grew.

"And here is Texas's station." Mon stopped a step back from the door, and my heart skipped a damn beat when Maya walked into view.

"Hey." She smiled shyly.

"Babe, what's goin' on?"

She shrugged, and I loved the way her cheeks heated. "You ramble on about the place. I thought I'd see it for myself."

Mon and Chris found this funny.

Grinning, I winked. "Glad to have you here. Come take a seat." I tipped my chin towards the couch in the corner. "I'm nearly done with Chris."

"Okay." She turned back to Mon. "Nice to meet you."

"Oh, believe me, the pleasure was all mine. Don't be a stranger." When Maya stepped through, I caught Mon behind her mouth, "Hot," while shaking her hand out in front of herself.

Rolling my eyes, I shifted my gaze back to Maya as she moved close to peek at what I was doing. "Maya, this is Chris. He's a regular from Melbourne."

"Hi, Chris."

"Hey, sweetheart."

Maya smiled, and I didn't miss the flare in Chris's eyes. Maya didn't see it because she was looking at Chris's tattoo.

"You like clowns?" Maya asked with no judgement in her tone.

Chris smirked. "I like anything horror."

"Cool." She nodded, and when she looked at me, her head cocked to the side. "Get to work, then."

Christ, why did her wanting to see me work get me nervous and excited? I didn't mind my gut playing havoc as long as the nerves didn't disrupt my hands in any way.

"Yes, boss."

As I started, Maya asked Chris, "Does it hurt?"

"There's a chance you'll see tears in my eyes. Look away if you do."

Maya's laugh was like music to my ears. "I will, promise. But can I ask, if it hurts so much, why get it done?"

"It'll be worth it in the end. Guess you don't have any ink?"

"Oh, um, no." I could feel her gaze on me, and hell, it made me want to puff up like a peacock.

"Reckon you'll get any?" Chris asked.

She hummed under her breath, and I glanced up to see her watching me. She blinked and straightened.

The blush was back.

Fucking cute.

"You mentioned you might," I said before changing the colour over in my gun.

"I'm still thinking about it. I wouldn't have a clue what to get if I did."

"Then it isn't the right time. I got this one, my first, after my pops passed away. Then I became addicted."

"I'm guessing there's a meaning behind the headless horseman?"

Chris snorted. "Yeah, when I was younger, we used to love reading about different folklores and decided that one was our favourite."

I caught Maya's warm smile before I got back to finishing the final touches.

"That's really sweet."

"That's me. Sweet."

I scoffed. "Don't let him fool you, babe. He's an arsehole."

Chris snorted again. "He's just a sore loser, sweetheart. Can't handle that I won a bet on drinking more than he could."

"Wait, seriously?"

"He cheated, babe. I would have won if he hadn't thrown that shot behind his damn head when I wasn't lookin'."

Maya laughed. "So, you've known each other a while?"

Chris nodded. "He did my first tattoo when he was an apprentice."

"You did the headless horseman?" Maya asked, voice high, like she couldn't believe it.

"Yeah." I nodded.

"When you were an apprentice?"

"Yep."

"Texas, you were that good even from the start, that's... amazing."

Fuck me, did it suddenly get hot in here?

I knew I was good. I knew I had a gift, but getting praises from Maya had me reacting like a schoolboy. My gut fluttered, my heart tripped, and heat flooded my cheeks.

"Aw, look, he's blushing," Chris teased.

Glaring, I finished the last bit while muttering, "I said before, Chris. Eat shit and die."

Both of them thought that was hilarious.

"So," Chris drew out. "How do you two know each other?"

"We go way back to when we were kids. Our families are close," Maya told him.

"Your dad a part of that club Texas is in?"

"Yeah." Maya smiled wide.

"Her dad's the big honcho."

Chris whistled. "Seriously?"

"He is."

"That's wicked."

I washed down his tattoo. The final was epic, even if I did say so myself.

Maya scoffed. "It'd be okay if I was Dad's son. Since I'm the daughter, he's a little overprotective. Dating has always been hard."

Chris chuckled. "You got anyone at the moment?"

I tensed. I knew the answer already, but I just didn't like the thought of Maya dating, full stop. But that was shit of me because I had a past too.

With a quick look at me, she shifted over to the couch and sat on the armrest. "No. No one."

"Well, I'm—"

"Chris," I warned.

His grin was full of mischief. "Yes, Texas?"

"Shut it." I nodded down at his leg. "You're done."

"Hell yes." He stood and went to the mirror. "Fuck, man. Another brilliant job."

"Thanks, man."

He shifted his leg around to face Maya. "What do you think, sweetheart?"

"Texas has real talent."

"Damn right he does." He jutted it out for me to wrap. "It's why I'd travel the damn world to get his ink. A lot of people who get tats try to find that perfect someone, and when we do, it's like a relationship you've got to keep."

I snorted and stood. "You in love with me, Chris?"

He let out an amused huff. "Nah man, just your hands." Chris walked towards the door. "I'll leave you two to it and fix the bill up with Mon at the counter."

"You got it. Till next time."

"Make sure you leave a spot open for me in six months," Chris called before he left. He already knew I would.

"I've just gotta clean up, and then I'm done. You wanna grab some dinner with me at my place?"

Say yes. Please, say yes.

Shit, there went my gut again.

"I, um.... Sure?"

She didn't sound certain. If anything—and I was going to guess—she was nervous.

Why did I want to grin like an idiot over it? Probably because it was good to know she was as nervous as I was. It was just that most of the time, I was better at hiding it.

As I set about cleaning, I asked, "Is there actually anythin' you don't eat? Like, I was gonna just throw some meat on the barbie. You good with that?"

"The only things I really can't stand are anchovies and olives. Other than that, I'm good. If you've got salad stuff, I can make one to go with the meat. Unless, with you being all tough and manly, you just want to stick with meat like a caveman would?" The little tilt to the corner of her lips was teasing.

"I got salad stuff, smartarse."

Her laugh always made me feel light on the inside.

While I cleaned, Maya stood up and made her way around the room, looking at pictures of old tattoos, then at the newer designs I had pinned to the wall that someone could pick to get inked. It really hit me in the chest when clients came in with a concept, only to then see one of my designs and fall in love with it and choose that instead.

Scrubbing things down took me longer than usual

because I kept watching Maya and pausing to answer any questions she had.

Finally, I started for the door and said, "All done. Let's get out of here."

"Um, Mon didn't really show me all of your shop. Would you?"

"Yeah, babe," I said gently, happiness fucking bubbling up.

I'd been having a good day already, but now that Maya was in my space, it got better and better. I couldn't wait to see how damn excited I'd be with her in my house.

There was a chance I wouldn't want her to leave.

CHAPTER NINETEEN

MAYA

*T*exas walked me down to the end of the hall and opened the door there. "This is the break room. It leads to the back door that opens to where Hex and Mon park." The room was your average lunchroom. To the right was the kitchenette. The table and chairs were in the middle, but then on the left, there was the one thing that stood out most. The whole wall was covered in a print that looked like it was an image from an alleyway in Melbourne, and down the alley, the walls were covered in cool graffiti.

"That is so cool. Who did it?"

"Emmy hooked me up with a guy she knows, since her and Warden were away at the time."

Emmy was Warden's wife, and Warden worked as a private investigator at my aunt's agency. "It's fantastic."

"Yeah, it turned out well." When he took my hand, I shivered and dropped my gaze down to it. "Come on, I'll show you the rest."

We walked back into the hallway. "The bathroom is on the left." We made our way towards the front of the shop. "My room, and then the one next to it is free, same as the two on the other side. But Mon's doing a course in piercings, so she'll pick one of those for herself. Might employ another couple of tattooists as well."

"Who's taking Mon's job?"

"Put out an ad for the position, but so far, those who have been in for an interview weren't the right fit." He shrugged. "I'll keep waiting." He stopped at the last door at the end of the hall before we hit reception and knocked.

"In."

Texas opened the door and the buzzing behind it stopped. A guy who was leaning over a client's shoulder lifted his head and grinned. He was covered in more ink than Texas because there wasn't a spot clear on his face. "Hey, you two." Why did his tone sound teasing?

"Hex, this is Maya. Maya, Hex, Mon's other half."

"Nice to meet you," I said, and glanced at the person on the bed.

Hex waved a hand. "He's got headphones on and is asleep."

My eyes near bugged out of my head. "He's asleep?"

Texas and Hex chuckled, but it was Hex who said, "Yeah, it happens sometimes."

"But... aren't.... Everyone says they're painful."

"Some people aren't bothered by the pain," Texas told me.

"Wow" was all I could say, which they found humorous.

Texas sent Hex a two-finger wave. "We'll leave you to it."

"You got it. Have a good night."

From the way he wiggled his eyebrows up and down, my face heated. It wasn't like Texas and I would get up to something scandalous. We could, and I'd like to. Instead, we were eating dinner together. A lot of people did it.

"Bye." I waved.

Texas closed the door and, with my hand still in his, led me into the reception area where Mon was sitting behind the desk, scrolling through things on the computer.

"Texas, I found the pieces of jewellery for the display cabinet."

"Great, order them. You know my details."

She nodded and turned her eyes to me, though I didn't miss when she briefly looked at our joined hands. "Maya, did he bore you with his work?"

"Not at all. It was fascinating."

"Good to hear. Hey, you should come in when I start up piercing. You'd look sexy with a nose ring."

My whole body warmed. "I don't know."

"What do you think, Texas? She'd look hot with one, right?"

Texas glared at Mon, but he still said, "She looks hot no matter what she does."

My mouth dropped open, and I stared up at Texas.

He just... he admitted... he thought I was hot.

I wasn't stupid. It was just taking me time to let the knowledge sink in that Texas liked me, but to hear him say something like that was like a bomb going off in my brain.

I snapped my mouth closed and looked away from Texas when I heard Mon's soft laugh. She winked at me before spinning back to the screen. "Anyway, I better get back to work. The boss is a dick."

"The boss can fire you for callin' him a dick," Texas grumbled as he pulled me along to walk around the desk and towards the front door.

"The boss would never do that because he loves me so much."

Texas snorted. "Like a hole in the head. Later, Mon."

"Bye, boss. See ya, Maya. Loved meeting you."

"You too," I managed to get out before the door closed. Texas took us to the house that joined the shop. "I still can't believe you live here," I said with a laugh, remembering when he told me about it on one of the many calls.

"Told you, it's all about luck." He let go of my hand to search his pockets for his keys.

"And at least there's no travel time for work."

"Exactly." He unlocked the front door, swung it open, and held his arm out.

I stepped through and waited off to the side for him to enter and close the door. My pulse picked up when he took my hand again as we made our way down the hall. Along the way, he explained each room. I had a glimpse into his and saw a queen-sized bed. One that was made.

At the end of the hall, we stepped into the open area for the kitchen, dining, and living area. I dropped his hand to turn in circles and take everything in.

"This house is huge." The rooms I'd looked in along the way were also big, but it was the living area that was spaced out perfectly. It held enough room for kids to run around while chasing chaos.

When he had them, of course.

"Some of it needs work. I want to paint a cool grey in here and redo the counters and cupboards."

"Grey would look great. You could get a splash of it in a white-and-black marble counter and white cupboards." I shut my mouth. "Sorry, for some reason I get excited about changing things in houses. Mum and Dad got sick of me wanting to redesign my room."

His smile was soft. "It's fine. I like the sound of it."

I had to look away before my gaze shifted down to his lips and locked in place.

Then he'd definitely know.

He would, right? Guys knew you wanted a kiss when you looked at their mouths?

I averted my eyes just as they started to slip down and

spun to face the kitchen. "Right, let's see what you have for your salad." I started towards the refrigerator. "Should I be scared to open it? Will anything jump out since it's a bachelor pad fridge?"

Texas's deep laugh followed me. "Nothin' to be scared of."

My heart rabbited behind my ribs when his body heat hit my back and he reached around me to open the refrigerator.

"See," he said quietly into my ear.

But my brain had shut down because he was close.

So, so close.

His chest was at my back. One of his hands was on my hip while the other held the door open.

If I pushed my butt back, would it find something hard?

Clearing my throat, I blinked and laughed nervously. "I guess you're a surprise."

"Maya."

Damn, that soft tone.

"Hmm?"

I wasn't really listening, too focused on trying to get my breathing under control. The last time I'd been this close to him was during that hug he gave me when I got home. The time before that was when I was sobbing into his chest. Both of those times, I never noticed how hard his chest was, but now that my back was pressed against it, my shoulder blades were screaming at me to find out for sure how firm his pecs were.

"Did you hear me?" he asked with the same gentleness.

One I wanted to hear when— Abort that thought.

"Um... no?"

His chuckle rocked my body. I had to get away, clear my mind so it would work better.

"Shift aside, babe. I'll grab the stuff."

"Okay." I nodded.

When I didn't move right away, his other hand touched my other hip, and he moved me to the side before he buried his head in the fridge. Meanwhile, I wanted to stuff mine in the freezer to cool it down.

I was sure I'd make a fool of myself by the end of the night and that Texas would know I wanted his lips on mine. If he didn't already.

Turning, I saw a chopping board and grabbed that, then a knife from his block to place them on his counter that faced the living area.

Being here, in his house, his domain, was dangerous.

I liked it too much already. Knowing we were going to make dinner together. Like we were a couple.

A jolt went through me when he placed the salad items on the counter at my side. "Thanks," I said, a little too high.

"You all right?"

"Yeah. Totally." I picked up the lettuce and started breaking pieces off to wash.

His hand rested down on my shoulder. "I'm gonna hit

the back deck and start cooking. How do you like your steak?"

"Well-done, please."

He gave my shoulder a squeeze. "You got it."

Jesus, it was like my lips were jealous of my shoulder. They wanted attention also.

No. They weren't allowed to get any. I wasn't completely sure he wanted a future with me anyway.

Yet the touches were coming more frequently. That meant something, right?

I quickly prepped the salad, which didn't take long, and by the time I was done, I didn't know what to do with myself. Did I walk out to him? Did I wait? Did I get myself a drink? Grab him a beer? Would it be rude to help myself? Would he care?

I took a deep breath and attempted to centre myself and my spiralling thoughts.

No, he wouldn't care. If it was Ruin or my brother, they'd help themselves to his drinks, and I didn't see the problem with me doing the same, since we were friends.

I grabbed a beer for Texas and myself a soda and then went out on the back patio. Texas hadn't heard me, and his back was to me, so I got to take him in without being caught. Slowly I slid my gaze over his arms covered in ink, then his shoulders and back, which were covered by his black tee and club vest. His butt and then legs were next. All parts of him I wouldn't mind touching.

"That drink for me?" came his amused voice.

My gaze shot up and straight into the window in front

of him, which I hadn't noticed before. It was connected to his shop that ran longer than the house. The blinds on the window were drawn, so he had a full view of my appraisal of him.

Shit.

"Um, yeah." I took the steps forward, but kept my distance, and thrust my arm out with his drink.

When he turned to take it, I looked down into the backyard. It was a good yard. A long one that was tidy and had a tree down the back where a garage was.

"Thanks."

"Hope you didn't mind me helping myself," I said to the wood under my feet.

Thankfully, he faced the barbeque again. "You can help yourself to anything you see and want."

Wait...

My brain had officially shut down.

Nope, it woke up again to shove images at me of kissing Texas. If I had enough courage, I would push him around and jump into his arms to slant my mouth over his.

But I couldn't conjure that courage up. Instead, my nerves skipped around on my insides.

Had he really meant what I thought he did?

I wasn't brave enough to ask.

I hated that I wasn't.

Texas saved me from my inner ramblings by asking how Drake and Ruby were. Even as I spoke, though, I couldn't stop thinking about taking that leap, all the while wishing he would make the first move. This in-between was slowly driving me crazy.

I *did* want to try this with Texas. I couldn't deny it. But would it be worth risking the friendship we'd found? What happened if we ended things badly? It wouldn't be good for us, obviously, but there were others to consider as well. Our families were close.

The thoughts had my stomach gurgling loudly.

Texas smirked. "How about we feed that beast before it comes alive?"

At least I could pass my nerves off as hunger.

"That would be good."

Okay, calm now, Maya. Stop staring at him and wishing things. It's probably too soon anyway. He might not be ready for me to know he has feelings, and I might not be ready to throw myself at him. Not that I'm going to because of my other worries about losing him from my life altogether, but is it bad if I ask if I can try before I buy?

Great, now I was rambling like Ivy did when she was nervous. At least it was silent, and I didn't actually ask if I could try him out beforehand.

Was that a thing though?

No. It really wasn't. Why was I even thinking such a thing?

"You wanna sit at the counter or the table?" Texas asked when we got inside.

"Up to you."

"Table it is. Grab the salad, babe."

After I found some plates and cutlery, I picked up the

salad and placed them all on the table. "Do we need placemats?"

Texas grinned but shook his head. We sat down and I dished up the salad while Texas placed a steak and chop on my plate.

If this wasn't domesticated, then I didn't know what was.

But God, it made me feel like I was floating.

I had to bite my bottom lip so he wouldn't see the wide and happy smile on my face that could come across as a scary grin that wanted out.

"Grab some more meat if you want," he said.

"I'm good, thanks." I cut into it. "It's cooked perfectly."

He snorted. "I can barbeque like the best of them. The rest I'm shit at."

I shrugged. "I'm all right in the kitchen. Nothing to brag about, though. I do like to bake, but now Channa's in our lives, she brings treats over all the time."

He groaned. "Her stuff is awesome."

"I can't argue with that. Did Dodge teach you to grill, or is it just something you picked up?"

"Dodge. He taught me a lot in life. I'll forever be grateful he came to get us when *she* died. Mum was a bitch, babe. Thankfully, I only had fourteen years with her and Rommy seven. Low's a good role model. Well, most of the time."

We shared a grin, but I lost mine. "Sorry you had a crap life with your mum, Texas."

He winked. "Worked out in the end." We finished dinner in silence, but it was comfortable. Even without any background noise.

After finishing, we rested back in our seats and talked about his work. How many clients he took on in a week, what Hex's style was, and how Mon was excited to set up her room.

When there was a break in conversation, I stood up and grabbed our dishes to clean off. Texas also climbed to his feet and grabbed the leftover meat and salad bowl.

We worked together in the kitchen while talking about random things.

I liked everything about what we were doing.

The time together.

The dinner and talking.

But especially the company.

Until the nerves flew back in after we'd cleaned everything, and I realised the polite thing to do would be to leave. He had work tomorrow. I didn't. Well, I did promise Dad I'd drop into the compound and clean up his office in the workshop. But other than that, I was a free lady. I could get up whenever I wanted, and Texas probably had an early client.

Standing in his kitchen, I rubbed my hands on my thighs and looked around while I said, "I, ah, better get going. Let you get some rest or get to your designing." I lifted my hand and waved lamely. "Night." I turned.

"Maya."

Pausing, I didn't look back, but I asked, "Yeah?"

"How about some ice cream?"

Facing him, I conjured up some sass and crossed my arms over my chest while raising a brow. "Don't you have work to do?"

His lips twitched. "Not right now."

"Oh, um, okay then."

"Good. Sit your arse up on the counter, and I'll dish some up."

I did, just so I could watch his body move around while he placed a couple of scoops of Neapolitan ice cream in the bowls. He passed one to me.

"I don't like Neapolitan."

He stilled, watching me, and I couldn't keep a straight face. He shook his head, smirking. "You're a shithead."

"Sometimes."

"Glad to see this side of you coming out more often," he said gently.

After stirring the ice cream around, I took a mouthful and shrugged. "I'm comfortable to be myself around you." Most of the time, that was. *Except when my wanton hussy comes out and wants to jump you.*

"Like that, babe."

I shrugged again, knowing my face was heating.

All too soon, my bowl was empty. Did I leave now? Texas stepped close and took my bowl from me. As he placed both next to me on the counter, my heart galloped under my ribs when he took another step closer.

"Maya."

"Hmm?" I asked, not daring to look up from his chest.

What was he going to say? Was he going to do something?

Gah, I screamed internally while butterflies took off in flight inside my stomach. Then they sped up into a tornado when his hands rested down on my thighs.

My breath caught in my throat as he gently shifted my thighs apart and stood between them.

"Maya."

"Y-Yes?"

"Look at me, gorgeous."

Oh. My. Fucking. God.

A shiver raked over me, but I slowly managed to lift my gaze to his. "Texas," I whispered.

His dark eyes ran over my face, and he tipped his chin up a fraction. "You know."

"Know what?"

"Know where this'll lead."

"Where?" I breathed as he leaned closer and slid his hand to the side of my neck. His thumb went under my chin, and he used it to tip my head up a little more.

"Here," he said against my lips.

CHAPTER TWENTY

TEXAS

ucking hell. I'd read the signals right. I'd seen her checking me out, and now I'd made my move.

The kiss started out as a soft brush of lips against each other's before we pulled back. Her eyes were wide and wild. Her fingers pressed into my hips.

I needed more.

I had to have more.

And when she licked her lips, I knew she wanted it too, and fuck, my cock thickened. Leaning in again, I brushed my mouth across the corner of hers.

"Texas," she whispered, her hands tightening on me again.

"Christ, babe," I got out before I nipped at her

bottom lip. Her mouth opened with a whimper, and I took my chance. I slanted my mouth over hers and turned the kiss into a hotter one that made her come alive in my arms. I got to taste, to suck, and tangle our tongues together. Her arms wound around my waist, her legs around my hips. I used my other hand, the one that wasn't at her neck, to thread my fingers through her thick hair and grip. Another whimper escaped her, and she dug her fingers into my back, dragging me closer, like she wanted inside me.

Hell, I wanted inside her. In every fucking way.

Her mouth was made for me. Her sounds were mine. I caused them. I brought those reactions out of her.

Fuck me.

She was giving me everything in this kiss. She was perfect.

But I had to stop this.

I couldn't take it too far.

I didn't want her to think this would be it.

All I needed was a taste, and I got it. And fucking loved it.

I broke the kiss to hug her tightly to me, holding her head to my chest. My hard cock was pressed into the cupboard between her legs. "Christ, Maya." I had to get her out of here. My restraint was lacking in my fog-kissed state.

Shit, I wanted her mouth again and again.

Stepping back, I helped her stand.

She blinked a little dazedly up at me. "Texas?"

Cupping her cheeks, I dipped back in for a quick taste. I couldn't stop myself. "I gotta get you home."

Her head jerked back. "What?" Anger flared in her eyes; the desire dropped away.

I smirked. "Babe, I gotta get you home or I'm gonna take you to my bed and fuck you like I've been picturing for months."

Crap. I hadn't meant to say that.

Maya's anger fled as she took heavy breaths. "Texas."

"It can't happen yet."

"Why not?" she demanded snappishly. Her attitude was just as much of a turn-on as everything else she did.

My grin at the thought faded as I pulled her close, staring down at her. "Because for once in my fuckin' life, I won't think with my dick. You deserve better. You deserve all the damn bells and whistles because you, Maya Marcus, are something special."

Tears formed in her eyes, and she dropped her forehead to my chest. "Shut up."

Chuckling, I kissed the top of her head. "I won't. You'll take care of this with me, what we have growin', yeah?"

"Are you sure—"

"Don't—fuck—please don't second-guess what I'm feelin'."

She lifted her head and met my gaze. "Okay, Texas."

"You wanna talk about this?"

"What?"

"Where this is goin?"

"I... um... I don't know. Yes, no, maybe. It's a lot." She looked away and then back again. "I never thought this could happen. I like how we've been."

Did that mean she wasn't sure about more?

Nah, fuck that—the kiss said she wanted me.

"I get that, babe. I do. We'll always keep what we've had, but it'll be so much more with what we have growin'. You trust me, yeah?"

"Yes, Texas." Good. Instant. Loved that.

"Just keep trustin' in me and know I'll take care of everythin' between us."

"You really want something more?"

"More than anythin' in my life."

She softened in my arms, sank into me, and Christ, she leaned in and kissed my chest. "All right, Texas."

"Good. Now, we're gonna go out on a date and talk some more tomorrow."

Her broad smile gripped my heart. "Can the date be here?"

"Not sure that's a good idea."

"Scared I'll jump your bones?"

I snorted out a wild laugh and wrapped her into a tighter hug. "Fuck, gorgeous. Love the shit you say."

"It could be true," she muttered.

"I believe you, which is why it could be dangerous havin' dinner here again."

She lifted up onto her tippy-toes and whispered in my ear, "Don't be scared, Texas. I'll be gentle."

Groaning, I put my hands on her hips and stepped

away from her before dropping my hands. "You're not makin' this easy." My cock throbbed behind its confinement.

Her laugh was carefree and more music to my ears. "All right, Texas. We'll play it your way."

"Good. Now let's get you home."

"I have my car, remember."

"Shit, I forgot. All right, I'll walk you to it." I took her hand and strode down the hallway. I needed to move swiftly past my bedroom or there was a chance I'd drag her in there. My fast pace was something Maya found funny. At the door, I swung it open and left it like that while we went across the street to her car. As I faced her, regret stabbed at my gut.

I didn't want to see her gone.

Reaching up, I gripped the back of her neck and pulled her close for the final kiss of the night. I knew the kiss would make it harder to let her leave, but I had to have her mouth again. It was already addictive.

"Fuck," I muttered against her plump lips. "Get in the car, babe."

"Okay," she said softly, but she didn't let go of my waist.

"Gorgeous, I need you to step back."

With a swift peck to my mouth, she unlocked her car and got in. As soon as it was started, she wound down her window.

"I was scared to take this leap, Texas. But I also knew I could never resist you. You've always been in my heart."

Before I could say anything, she wound up her window and I shifted back in time for her to pull out and drive off.

You've always been in my heart.

Holy hell. Those words were like a punch to the heart in the best kind of way.

EVEN THE NEXT day I couldn't get her words off my mind. The hours ticked by at a snail's pace. Work didn't seem to distract me like it usually did either. Not that I didn't put my full effort into my jobs. I did and always would. But it felt like there were ten days in the single one with how long it lasted.

After I cleaned my station, I made my way out to the front where Mon was. Her teasing grin annoyed me. She knew I was going on a date that night. It had slipped out when she was pestering me about Maya that morning.

"Only an hour to go until you see her. You excited?"

"Mon, I'll give you ten dollars to shut it." My gut was already twisting with nerves. Never had them like I did with Maya, but there was a lot riding on the night.

While Mon laughed, I went to the computer and looked at tomorrow's schedule. I already had Elisabeth's and James's designs ready, and they were my morning clients. I could finish the touches on Oliver's on my break. Thank fuck there was nothing going on within the club that was an urgent matter and had us too busy for other things. I knew it could happen, even at the drop of a hat. If it did, I'd push clients back or get them in with someone else I trusted, because the club came first. Along with Maya.

"How's our boy doing?" I heard Hex ask.

"He's distracting himself until he goes to pick up his woman," Mon answered.

"Do you think we need to have the birds-and-the-bees talk with him?"

Why did I employ them?

Mon hummed. "I think it could be a good idea. Do you have any condoms we can give him?"

"Don't even fuckin' try it," I warned. Of course, they found that amusing.

"Stop stressing," Hex said with a pat to my shoulder. "She already likes you. I'm sure you can't fuck this up."

"Well," Mon drew out. I shot her a glare, causing her to laugh and hold her hands up. "I'm kidding. Where are you taking her?"

"I'm not telling you. You'll probably turn up just to annoy me."

She tried for an innocent look. "Who, me?"

Shaking my head, I straightened. "I'll see you both tomorrow."

Mon grinned. "Just call me if you can't make it in."

"Don't forget to wrap it before you tap—" Hex took a step back from the look I shot him. "I'll shut up now."

Grunting, I walked around the counter and out the

front door. Usually, I didn't mind their teasing. But I just wasn't having it because it was Maya. The women from my past, I didn't care about. Maya, I did.

Once home, I took a quick shower and changed into my dark jeans, a long-sleeve black top, my club vest, and boots. I wasn't taking my bike to pick Maya up. Though, having her wrapped around my back sounded appealing. Instead, I wanted to hold her damn hand like we were teens.

On the drive over, I cracked my neck, relieved I'd already talked to Talon. It meant if he was home, he already knew my intentions and had given me his approval. However, it wouldn't surprise me if I got some type of fresh warning before taking Maya out.

At the door, I knocked and heard Drake yell, "I'll get it." His footsteps pounded from inside and then the door swung open. "Hey, Texas." He moved back.

"How's it goin', kid?"

"Good, good." He nodded and then turned to the hall. "Maya, Texas is here for your date." He sang the last word loudly.

"Drake," she yelled, her tone full of warning.

Drake rolled his eyes and then shut the door. He stood beside me, crossing his arms over his chest. "Right," he drew out, "Dad ain't home, so you got me to deal with. I'm guessin' you already know the talk, but I'm still gonna give it to you straight. You hurt my sister in any fuckin' way, I will hunt you down and make you pay in the worst way possible. Got it?"

I looked down at the floor while my lips twitched. Blanking my expression, I met his hard, serious gaze, then nodded. "Got it, Drake."

He gave me a friendly smile. "Great." With a slap to the back, he nodded towards the couch. "Wanna sit while you wait? God only knows how long she'll take."

"I'm here," Maya called before she hit the living room. When she did, my throat closed over and I forgot how to breathe.

"Fuck," I muttered.

Drake chuckled, rolled his eyes, and went to lounge on the couch.

Maya's sweet smile had me sucking in air and then returning it with an open-mouthed, crazed one.

She was going to be mine and she knew it.

Christ, I was a lucky guy.

"Maya," slipped out softly when she stopped in front of me. "Jesus, babe, you look stunnin'." I'd thought I'd seen her in everything she owned.

I hadn't.

It would have been burned into my brain if she'd ever worn this red dress. One that was cut just above her knees, sleeveless, and hugged her body like a second skin.

"It's not too much?"

"No," I said instantly. Reaching out, I placed a hand on her waist, leaned in, and took her mouth like I'd been thinking of doing all day. She melted into me. Her hands went to my chest and slid up to wind around my neck.

Drake dry retched in the background, but I couldn't

break the kiss. At least I refrained from palming her arse like I wanted to.

A throat cleared.

It was only then I broke the kiss and glanced to the side.

Damn me and my impulsive ways.

Talon and Zara stood inside the doorway. At least Zara was smiling, while Talon, my prez, looked at me like he wanted to rip me apart.

I could understand why. I did have my tongue down his daughter's throat. I'd be pissed too if I saw it happen to my daughter, if I had one.

Maya shifted so she was in front of me. "Mum, Dad. Hey. You guys are back early."

"It's all right, Dad. I gave him the talk," Drake called.

Maya spun his way so she was at my side. "What talk?"

"Just know Texas and I have an understandin'."

She snapped her gaze up to me. "What understanding?"

Grinning, I tapped her nose. "Nothin' you need to worry about, gorgeous."

"Texas knows where I stand," Talon said.

Maya turned to him. "What do *you* mean?"

Talon smiled, and it was a little scary. "Just some little threats among brothers."

"You—"

I curled my arm around Maya's waist and brought her against me. "Relax, babe. It's all good. They're just keepin' an eye out for you."

She harrumphed. "Fine."

"Curfew's at midnight," Talon ordered gruffly.

"Dad, I'm twenty-freaking-one. I don't have a damn curfew."

"Honey." Zara pushed herself into her man. "Leave them be." She looked at us. "Just go and have a good date."

Talon pointed to his eyes and then to me. I nodded in return, fully understanding I held his precious cargo in my hands and was to take the utmost care of her. Which I would. Maya wasn't only his to take care of, to guard, to cherish.

She was mine.

CHAPTER TWENTY-ONE

aya

DINNER WAS at a restaurant in town. It was a small and cute one that I'd never been to. More importantly, it wasn't loud and busy, which meant it was the perfect place for us to talk without having to yell over other people.

We'd just ordered and the waitress had disappeared when Texas's attention locked on me. "Gonna say it again, babe. You look damn stunnin'."

My body warmed like it had at the house when he'd said the words the first time. "Thanks."

"Not that you don't look hot all the other times, Maya. You do. It's just the red against your skin, and with your hair down and curled more... fuck."

A nervous laugh left me. I couldn't deny that Texas

was attracted to me. I just needed time to get used to it and that we were on a date. We'd also kissed. And we were going to be an *us*.

I wasn't dreaming. This was happening.

All day I'd freaked out that I'd been too forward the previous night by pretty much admitting I would have stayed to sleep with him. And without a doubt or regret, I would have, because as soon as he'd kissed me, it was like a wave of desire rocked straight into my body. For a brief moment, I'd even considered stripping naked and begging, but my sanity had shot back, and I'd realised I was in the same boat as Texas. I didn't want to rush... yet. Though, technically, it was a new day, so did that mean it was new rules?

"You look good too, Texas. You always do."

"Babe." It was a soft babe. One I loved hearing.

I picked at my napkin while I said, "I really like your ink, and the way you dress, and your hair on your head and face." God, that sounded lame, and yet I still finished with, "It's hot."

"Babe." That babe was a bit tighter and had me looking up at him. My breath caught, my pulse raced, and my stomach dipped. The heat in his eyes made them look darker than normal. I jumped when he suddenly got out of his chair and came at me. He dug his fingers into my hair to pull my head back so he could kiss my next breath away. When we stopped, I was left panting.

"Texas," I whispered. I didn't look around, but I knew people were watching. I didn't care, though.

"When you say shit like that, it's gonna make me want to kiss you, so expect me to do just that, no matter where we are." His tone was rough and caused me to shiver.

"Okay."

"Good." With a peck to my lips, he moved back to his seat and sat. "Now, we're gonna talk."

I nodded. It was all I could manage, still a little lost from that kiss.

"Maya, I fucked up when it came to you in the past."

I stilled and pressed a hand over my belly.

"I want you to know it won't ever happen again. I should have seen you back then. I didn't, and that was the biggest mistake I made. But I see you now, babe. I've seen you for a fuckin' long time."

My insides turned buttery as he continued, "You give me your heart and I'll take care of it in a way where you won't ever have to worry about me or my intentions because you'll know what I want. And, Maya, what I want is you in my life as mine. My woman. My old lady."

Oh.

My.

God.

Tears formed in my eyes, and I bit my bottom lip to stop it from trembling.

"I know we've got a lot of time to lead up to the final point where I put a ring on your finger, but you gotta know, babe, that I see no one else but you in my future. Are you willing to hop on this ride with me and see where this can take us?"

"Texas," I uttered, and slammed my lips into a tight line, afraid I was about to cry. I slid my gaze to the side and sucked in some deep breaths through my nose.

"Did I fuck up? Did I say this at the wrong time? Do you not want long term with me?"

Standing up, I wiped at my eyes as I walked to his side and pushed at his shoulder until he skidded his seat back so I could sit on his lap and curl into him.

My arms were so tight around him, I worried I'd strangle him. When I lifted my head from his shoulder and he cupped my cheeks, I drew in a shuddering breath. "I'm ready to hop on that ride with you, Texas."

"Christ," he clipped before he kissed me once again.

Something was placed on the table. I pulled back from Texas with a bright smile before I glanced to the side and found our waitress putting our food down.

I went to get up from Texas's lap, but his arm tightened around my waist.

As I turned back to him, he kissed the corner of my mouth, my nose, and cheek. "Made me a fuckin' happy man, babe."

"The feeling is mutual," I told him softly.

"Let's get some food into you. Heard women can get testy if they're not fed regularly."

Snorting, I shoved his shoulder as I stood and went back to my seat. "I can't deny it, but shouldn't this be something you already know?"

"The only women I've been around in any long-term

situation are Low and Rommy. Low's already testy about everythin', and Rommy's too sweet to get testy."

The only women he'd been around for a long period of time were his family.

Hadn't he had other long-lasting girlfriends?

"But—"

"None of those girls I was with mattered, Maya."

"But—"

"They were fillers because I knew they weren't right for me. Who *is* right for me has been right in front of me for nearly my whole life, but I didn't have my fuckin' eyes open."

"Shut up."

"Maya—"

"Please, I can't take anymore sweetness or I'll cry, and then I can't enjoy my meal."

He smirked. "All right, babe, I'll shut up for now."

"Thank you."

I BOUNCED my knee up and down as Texas drove along the road. Dinner was amazing. His words were beyond that. Now he was taking me home, but I didn't want to go home. I just didn't know how to tell him, worried it was too soon.

But I couldn't stop thinking about the fact that I'd been waiting for him to see me since I was sixteen.

Hadn't I waited enough? I thought I had.

Besides, he wanted a future with me. He'd said so himself.

"Texas."

His tattoo-covered hand on my thigh squeezed. "Right here, babe."

I covered his hand with mine and played with his rings. Softly, I asked, "Can I stay the night at your place?"

The car swerved to the right, but Texas got it under control again with both hands on the wheel. "Say again?"

"Um, can I stay at your place? I know you said to go slow, that you don't want to think with your dick, and want to give me all the bells and whistles, but, Texas, I've wanted you for a *long* time."

I didn't like his pause; it made me feel like I was being too forward again, and doubt started to creep in.

"Text your mum. Can't have my woman waitin' any longer," he told me in a harder tone, and I watched him grip the wheel tighter before he turned it around towards his place.

I did as he requested, and it quickly chimed back.

MUM:

Okay, sweetie. Have fun.

She sent it with a winky face emoji.

I placed my phone in my bag again and held it on my

lap. I wanted to know what Texas was thinking, so I asked him.

"I'll be honest, babe. I'm worried that when I get you home, I'll have you on your back in a second because I've been thinkin' about eatin' you before I fuck you."

My mouth dropped open and a mew-like sound escaped. I pressed my thighs together, feeling my panties get wet.

Texas snapped his gaze down to my legs and gripped the wheel again. "Fuck. You're down with that thought, aren't you?"

I didn't say anything.

I couldn't.

Texas glanced over at me. "Yeah, you're down with that. Christ, Maya. I can't fuckin' wait to get my hands on you. I'm gonna strip you bare and pleasure every damn inch of you, just like you deserve." He stopped the car and jumped out.

I blinked slowly and noticed we were parked out the back of Texas's place. Next, my door was yanked open. Texas reached in and undid my seat belt before he picked me up and flung me over his shoulder.

"Texas!"

"Shush. Gotta get my woman inside to take care of her."

A moan slipped free when he ran a hand up and under my dress to caress my butt cheek. I heard the door being roughly unlocked and opened. A light flashed and I was placed on my feet as Texas shut the door and locked it again.

He spun on me, picked me up again, but this time he pressed my front to his. Immediately, I wound my arms around his neck and legs around his hips.

That was when I felt it.

Just how turned-on Texas was.

He really had been thinking of doing those things to me.

Unable to help myself, I sucked on his neck, and I lifted my body up a little so I could press my crotch in and rub over his erection. Texas massaged my arse, pushing me against him more. I drew in a ragged breath at the sensation of my clit getting teased.

"Jesus Christ, babe." He kicked at a door, then stepped into his bedroom. "Down, Maya," he said gruffly. I dropped to my feet and reached behind me to undo the zip on the dress. Texas's eyes flared and heated more. He took off his vest and put it on the hook behind his door. His tee was next, but that went to the floor.

I managed to get my zip down, only to stop moving while I watched the show in front of me.

Texas's hand went to his button, then the zipper. Both came undone as he kicked off his boots. His socks were next before he straightened and hooked his thumbs into the sides of his jeans and pushed them down his legs, revealing more tattoos. So many more.

Swallowing thickly, I took in his body and frowned

when I noticed he still wore boxers. Tented boxers, but they were hiding what I really wanted to see.

"Babe." My tone held a little frustration.

"Hmm?"

I waved a hand his way. "Are you going to remove those?"

He chuckled. "When you catch up to me."

I lifted my head and saw his amusement-lit eyes. They dropped to my clothes.

Oh, I was still dressed.

Smiling, I slipped the dress from my shoulders. When it pooled at my feet, I kicked it, and my heels, away.

"Fuck," Texas clipped, his burning eyes on my black lace panties and bra. I'd worn them as a "just in case", and I was glad I did. Texas cursed again and scrubbed a hand over his face.

I reached around once again and got my hands on my bra latch.

"Wait," Texas ordered. I dropped my arms and watched him step close to cup each breast. "Babe, one thing you gotta know. I'm a tit man," he told my breasts. "And these beauties are the best I've fuckin' seen." He dipped down, eyes still raised up to mine while he took my right nipple between his teeth. I sucked in a sharp breath. He did the same to the other and my knees grew weak. "I ain't fuckin' lyin', gorgeous." He reached around me and unhooked my bra smoothly, slowly dragging the straps down my arms. His gaze was glued to my chest at the unveiling, giving him a clear sight of them.

He groaned and cupped both to feel their weight. Leaning down again, Texas licked around my left nipple and then sucked it in, driving me into a frenzy. I had to grab a hold of his upper arms or I'd fall.

"Texas, please," I breathed.

"What, Maya?"

I snuck a hand between us and wrapped it around his boxer-clad erection. He hissed out a breath, cooling my wet nipple.

"Need you," I said as I let go of him to shove his boxers down his legs so I could see what was in store for me. What I saw had me swallowing.

He was long and thick. I wasn't completely inexperienced, but I already knew it would take some time for it to fit all the way in.

And then I was distracted.

My head rocked back, my mouth opened, and I moaned when fingers found their way inside my panties *and* me. I'd been too busy studying him that I didn't see or feel him move until I *felt* him.

"Goddamn, baby. How're you gonna react when I fill you?" His voice was a low grumble, and then his lips, teeth, and tongue attacked my neck while his fingers played through my wetness. "Christ, so wet and tight."

I spread my legs more, even though they shook, and tightened my hand around him, fisting up and down over his length, dragging out a groan. I let out a sound of complaint when I lost his fingers, and then I had to let go of him all together because he picked me up once more.

"Bed," he said against my lips. I opened up to a hot and heavy kiss while he lay me down on his sheets, covering me with his body. His mouth moved down my neck to my breast, but only for a moment, because next he stood up and dragged my panties down my legs. "Open for me, babe. I'm hungry for a taste."

Panting, I nodded and slowly spread my legs for him. Ignoring the blush from feeling exposed, I wanted to do this for Texas. Not only because he'd asked, but because he already had my body humming with desire. I wanted everything he offered.

He climbed back onto the bed and settled between my legs. He planted a kiss to each thigh, to my stomach, my mound.

"Babe, you have me starvin'." He tucked his hands under me, and he lifted me up to his mouth where he swiped the full length of my opening with his tongue, groaning.

"Texas," I cried, gripping the sheets at my sides. He kissed, licked, and then flicked his tongue everywhere. Already my lower belly tingled. My toes curled. "Oh God."

He latched his mouth around my clit and slid his tongue up and down over it. I closed my eyes, back arching as I drew closer to a release.

He lowered me to the bed but kept up playing over my clit while a finger or two glided in and out of me. Stretching me.

"Christ, baby. So damn tight."

I glanced down to see him watching his fingers enter in and out. Seeing him staring with such a look of lust drove me closer to the edge—until I shattered around his fingers when he flicked his tongue over my clit again.

Breathing harder, I pressed a hand to my chest and opened my eyes to see Texas, orbs so dark and filled with more hunger, hovering over me. When he shifted to the side, I heard a drawer open, a crinkle of wrapper, and then he leaned back to kneel between my legs.

My pussy spasmed from witnessing him rip the condom with his teeth and slide that sucker down over his length. His warmth covered me again. I reached for him, running my hands up and down his sides. Our gazes locked, and I felt his hand between us, lining himself up. He brought it out to slap down on the bed beside my head, and he slowly pushed in.

Leaning down, he touched his lips to my nose, my cheek, my lips, and forehead as he edged in further. "Fuck, baby. You good?"

"Yeah," I got out a bit shakily. "You're just big."

"You have had—"

I nodded. "Once."

"Once?" When I nodded again, he cursed. "Let me know if I hurt you. I'll stop."

"Texas, I'm not breakable. I'll be fine." I opened my legs more and reached down to grip his arse. Lifting my top half up a little, I nipped at his chin. "Fuck me, baby."

He groaned and slid all the way in.

"Harder," I demanded.

"Babe—"

I cupped the back of his head and dragged him down for a kiss. He grunted into my mouth and then pulled his hips back to thrust into me. I dragged my nails over his skin. He must have taken it as encouragement, just the way I meant it, because he pulled back again to slam in.

I broke the kiss to cry, "Yes, baby."

Then it was on. We were all over each other—hands, teeth, mouths, and tongues. Each time he entered me, it was a little harder, and I freaking loved it. I lifted my hips, meeting his while he pressed in and rolled, teasing my clit.

The wet sounds were erotic. But we got off on it. We were made to fuck. Made to take each other. He fit in my body amazingly. His thickness sat snugly inside me where I felt *all of him.*

I dug my fingers into his arse again, my toes curling once more as my belly tingled. "Texas, God, yes, please."

"Fuck, babe. Fuck. Close."

"Yes. Now," I drew out as another orgasm crashed through me and my pussy clamped around him.

He grunted, burying his forehead into my shoulder to groan. His thrusts faltered a little as his muscles became taut, and with a moan, he emptied into the condom.

After a sweet kiss to my neck, he slumped to the side, both of us trying to find more oxygen.

"That," I panted. "Was. Epic."

An abrupt chuckle left him. He curled me into him and kissed my cheek. "Because it was us together."

My body melted. "Yeah," I whispered.

CHAPTER TWENTY-TWO

MAYA

a phone rang. I stretched and realised there was something heavy hanging over my waist. Not only that, but I was naked and achy, in a good way, between my legs. Then the night before strolled back into my mind, and I smiled.

Texas's heat disappeared from my back for a moment, and I heard him slap his hand to the bedside table. "Yeah?" he answered. Last night, he'd gotten up to lock the house down, turn off the lights, and grabbed my bag and his phone to bring them into the bedroom with a couple of bottles of water.

Texas sat. "Shit, what time is it?... All right, tell her I'll be there in half an hour.... Mon, I said half an hour.... If she's not happy, we can reschedule. Thanks." He hung up and crashed back down beside me. His arm curled under me, and he pulled me over him until I was lying on top of his deliciously naked body.

He grinned up at me. "Mornin', babe."

My stomach fluttered. God, he was good-looking. "Morning." I dipped down and kissed him. It was only supposed to be a quick kiss, but it led to more. I pushed against his chest. "Wait, who was that on the phone?"

"Seems we slept later than I thought we would." That was what he got for not setting an alarm. When I'd mentioned he should, he told me his body clock always woke him up on time.

"That was your fault for waking me in the middle of the night."

His grin turned smug. "You didn't complain when I slid inside you."

"Well... no." I smacked his chest. "Stop distracting me. Are you supposed to be at work?"

"If I say yes, what are you gonna do?"

I pushed at him to let me go, which caused me to slide down his body a little, only stopping when his morning wood nestled between my legs. I gasped, and he smirked. Licking my lips, I shook my head and cleared my throat. "Texas, you have someone waiting on you. Please let go."

He rocked up against me. "That's what I don't want to do."

"Texas," I managed to snap. I really didn't want him to lose a client because of us being up too late. "This is your livelihood; you don't want to upset a customer."

"I do if I have to let you go and then we won't get to shower or have breakfast together like I planned in my head last night."

I stopped pushing against him and relaxed down over him, resting my hands on his chest to lay my chin on them. Sighing, I arched up when an idea hit me. "How about you go shower and get to work. I'll run home to shower and get a change of clothes, then I'll come back with coffee and breakfast for you at work?"

"And miss the chance to shower together?"

Leaning in, I kissed him and then said, "There'll be many other chances to shower together."

"Like tonight?"

Laughing, I shook my head and then shrugged. "I'll have to see. Come on, you can't keep your work waiting for much longer."

He groaned and kissed me as he rolled us to our sides. "I'll see you soon?"

"Yes."

"Drive safe."

I nodded. "I will. Go shower."

His lips thinned. While he didn't want to, he would because I asked, and deep down, he knew I was right. My heart skipped and belly went crazy again. He grumbled as he climbed out of bed and walked naked to his en suite. Of course, I watched him go. I wasn't missing the show. When I heard the shower turn on, I forced myself to get out of the warm bed. Smiling as I dressed, I felt light. A shiver swept over me as I thought about what we'd done in that bed, only to cringe when I realised I would have to go home in last night's clothes.

God, I hoped Dad was already at work.

THANKFULLY WHEN I GOT HOME, no one was there. I took a shower and dressed in jeans, a simple off-the-shoulder black sweater, and ballet flats. Since Channa's wasn't too far from Texas's, I decided to go there.

During the drive, I couldn't stop thinking about Texas. Last night had been amazing. After my one previous experience, I'd never thought sex could be as good as what I'd heard some women talk about. Texas showed me it could be mind-blowing, and I honestly couldn't wait for it to happen again. Even thinking about the next time had me all warm and tingly.

As I drove, my phone rang, and since it was connected to the car already, I pushed the button to answer Easton's call. We'd grown closer when I started working as a paramedic, but more so after what had happened.

"Hi, Easton."

"Hey, Maya. What are you up to today?"

"Just heading to Channa's bakery and grabbing some breakfast to take to Texas at his work."

He groaned. "Boy, would I love some of Channa's muffins right about now." I heard laughter in the background. "Shut up, Parker. You know that's not what I meant."

Snorting, I grinned.

"Ignore the childishness in the background, Maya. Are you doing anything after that?"

"I have a free afternoon." But tonight I wanted to spend with Texas. My heart gave off an extra beat in agreement.

"Parker, Lan, and I are coming to Ballarat. Lan's going to see his cousin, and I was wondering if you... I mean, you don't have to, but I thought it might be good to see some people at the depot."

My pulse raced, and I quickly slowed to pull over down the street from Channa's. I pressed a hand over my heart as my stomach clenched.

I needed to make a decision about work. Not only had I forced the thought of work away, but also the people there. They'd tried to reach out. They'd tried to be there for me. But I wasn't handling life well at the time they made contact, and then when I could, they'd stopped trying, and I never returned their calls or texts. Guilt twisted inside me. The depot and the people reminded me too much of what I'd lost in one night. Not only John, but the way I'd felt safe.

Still, maybe I'd put off going there long enough. With Easton by my side, some of my stress would be eased more so than it would by arriving on my own.

"Maya? You don't have to. I'm not pushing you to go there."

"It's okay. I-I want to, but... I still don't know if I want to work there in the end." Did that make me a chicken? If I quit, did it make me weak?

"Honey, you don't have to choose. Not now. Not in a week. Only when you're ready."

He was right that I had pretty much indefinite leave, considering the attack happened during work time. Knowing work wasn't forcing me to return helped me breathe easier.

"You'll stick with me?"

"Like glue."

"It's not that I don't like the people there," I added quickly.

"But it can be overwhelming. I get it."

"I'd like to go with you, Easton."

"Okay, honey. Do you want me to pick you up from Texas's work or will you be home?"

"His work, please."

"You got it. I already know where it is. I'll be there around three."

"Thanks."

"And, Maya, even if we arrive at the depot and you don't want to go in—that's all right too."

"All right," I whispered with a nod. We ended the call, and I stared out the window towards Channa's bakery, thinking that this would be good for me. It wasn't long ago when Devlin suggested a visit to work, saying it could help me make up my mind so I could make a decision about my future. At the time, I'd shot the thought down.

Now, I clung to the small amount of strength to help me get through this and hopefully come out in the end with a plan.

Drawing in a deep breath, I ignored the rising anxiety by biting down on my bottom lip and pulled out to park closer to Channa's.

The bell jingled as I entered. Channa glanced over from behind the counter and greeted me with a warm smile before she went back to serving her current customer. A lot of the tables were full, which didn't surprise me because the food was delicious.

"Hey, Maya," Denise called. She worked with Channa and was also a good friend of hers.

"Hi, Denise."

"What can I get you?"

Before I could answer, we all heard someone yell, "I don't care what you say! We're doing it my way."

"Stanley, I will kick you in the balls if you touch my cupcakes." That was Susan, another employee like Stanley. Both of them were a little older, and you wouldn't think it, but they liked each other a lot.

Channa stuck her head out the back. "Will you two keep it down?"

"No," they both snapped back.

Channa sighed and walked our way. Her face brightened once more. "Maya, how did your date go?"

"Date?" Denise asked. "Oooh, do tell. Who was it with?"

Channa gave me a tight smile and mouthed, "Sorry."

I waved her off. Thinking and even talking about Texas was a good distraction from what I had to do this afternoon.

"Denise, I'm not sure if you've met Texas before, but—"

"Have I met Texas, that hunk of tattooed man meat? Yes, I have. You went on a date with him?"

Laughing, I nodded. "Yes, and it went well." I glanced at Channa and found her smiling softly. I asked, "I guess someone told Cody about it?"

"Yes. He was on the phone last night with Drake."

That explained it. Drake had a big mouth.

"Now, did you pop in for a visit or do you need some things?" Channa asked.

"Actually, I'm taking brunch to Texas at his work."

"That's a good sign," Denise said.

Channa nodded. "A very good sign. I'm happy for you. Hey, maybe we could do the double date thing again."

"Wait, so you've already been on a date with Texas?" Denise asked.

I shook my head "No. It.... Well, Channa mentioned a band when we'd all been together and we all decided to go, but it wasn't a date."

"Ah," Denise drew out. The bell jingled as some customers left and others entered. Denise walked over near the register to greet them.

"What are you going to take?" Channa asked.

I glanced along the counter. "I'm thinking a mixture

of things. Some muffins, a couple of bacon-and-egg burgers, and cookies?"

"Sounds good. I'll get it ready. Won't be long." She leaned in closer. "And sorry again for saying anything in front of Denise."

I gave her a reassuring smile. "Don't worry about it. Texas and I, well—we're actually dating now."

Her eyes widened, and she let out a squeal while jumping on the spot. "That's the best news."

"I think so too."

"Aww, that look on your face says it all. You're smitten."

I was.

How could I not be?

It was Texas.

My body warmed as I thought of him.

Channa laughed. "Okay, all right, I'll get your stuff together so you can get back to him."

"Can you add in a couple of egg-and-bacon rolls for his co-workers? Oh, and four cappuccinos, please."

She winked. "You got it." When she disappeared to the back, I snuck over to the register, since Denise was done with her customer.

"Can you ring me up?" I told her what I was getting and then paid. I knew Channa wouldn't charge me because I was her man's sister, but I wanted to pay. She had workers to take care of. "Don't tell Channa I paid."

Denise shared a smile with me. "Your mum does the same thing."

Laughing, I shrugged. "Doesn't surprise me."

By the time I got the items, it was nearing lunchtime, and as I thought, Channa had waved me off when I went to pay. I called out a "Thank-you" and went on my way.

I wasn't sure why, but in that moment, I was more nervous about seeing Texas than the afternoon adventure. My pulse sped under my skin, and by the time I stopped out the front of his shop, parking on the opposite side of the road, I'd started to sweat a little.

Blowing out a breath, I flung the strap of my bag over my shoulder, grabbed the box, and hooked the plastic bag over my wrist before I kicked my door open and climbed out. I used my hip to shut the door and beeped the locks.

"Okay, you've got this. You've already kissed, seen each other naked, and *know* he's into you," I told myself as I made my way across the street.

CHAPTER TWENTY-THREE

TEXAS

$\mathcal{J}$ wished I was back in bed with Maya. I loved my job. Loved it. But I already missed Maya. Closing my eyes for a beat, I stretched and clenched my teeth. I'd worked on Elizabeth before, and last time she wasn't as squirmy, but then again, that tat was on her arm, while this one was on her calf, and her leg kept twitching. It was starting to annoy me, but I kept at it while trying to hold her leg still.

"Remind me to never get another one on my leg," Elizabeth complained.

Chuckling, I nodded. "Arms are always out in the sun more than legs. The skin tends to be tougher. Don't worry. I'm nearly done." Thank fuck. It wasn't that I didn't enjoy doing this tattoo either. I just wanted my eyes on Maya again. The night and morning had gone too fast, and I hadn't had my fill of her. However, it was something I'd have to deal with because no matter how much we saw each other, I doubted I'd ever get enough.

A knock sounded on the door and my gut spun. "Yeah?"

Mon appeared. "Oh, don't frown at me. Your girl's here in the break room. She didn't want to interrupt you working."

I snorted. "Tell her to get her arse in here."

Mon grinned. "Will do." She leaned out the door and called, "Maya, get your arse in here before he shits a haemorrhoid."

Elizabeth thought that was hilarious.

Maya peeked her head around. "Hi." She waved, her gaze flicking to Elizabeth and back to me. I hoped she didn't mind that I tattooed women as well. It meant nothing to me. They were and would always be work. Even when I first started and women tried to hit me up, I declined them all. It was never good to mix pleasure with business.

Besides, no one else made my chest ache at the sight of them.

It was mind-blowing knowing that she was mine.

Finally mine.

"Babe, grab your breakfast and sit on the couch."

"I'll wait until you can eat."

"Babe."

"Texas," she mimicked.

I ignored the monkeys watching us with amused smirks.

"Maya, please come and eat in here while I finish up. I like knowing where you're at when you're here."

Her eyes warmed before she nodded.

I winked at her before she left, then turned my gaze to my employee. "Mon, get back to work."

She rolled her eyes. "Fine, but I thought you should know I'm half in love with her. She brought Hex and me coffees and food. You make sure you keep her."

Shaking my head, I grinned. "Planning to."

"Aww," she cooed, and then moved off shouting, "Hex, our boy really is growing up."

"Shut the fuck up," I yelled.

Maya appeared again with a coffee and bag in hand. She gave me a sweet smile and went to the couch, but before she sat, I called, "Babe, come here."

She put her items on the desk next to the couch and turned to me. "What?"

"Come here."

Her brows dipped in confusion, but she walked my way and stopped, looking down at Elizabeth's job. Vines ran up and down the side of her calf.

"That looks amazing," she told Elizabeth.

"Thanks. It hurts like a bitch, though."

Maya winced. "Sorry to hear that."

"Babe."

She lifted her gaze to me. "Yes?"

I tipped my chin at her. She moved around the table and got close. "Kiss me," I ordered.

"Texas," she snapped low, glancing quickly at Elizabeth, then back.

Elizabeth grinned. "Don't mind me."

I wouldn't, and hopefully, Maya didn't either. "Hurry up, babe. I gotta get this done."

She glared. "Then get it done."

"Maya."

She let out a frustrated breath, leaned in, and brushed her lips against mine. Then quickly made her way back to the couch where she sat down and kept her scowl on me. I knew what that glare was about. She'd be worried about doing it in front of a customer. But this was the long haul for us, and my woman would eventually understand that nothing else mattered but us. When I saw her, I wanted her taste back on me.

"All right, Elizabeth. You ready?"

"No. Yes." She closed her eyes and leaned her head back. My gun buzzed to life, and I finished what I had to do while my woman sat in the room, watching, eating, and drinking. Christ, I loved having her here.

It was after Elizabeth left and I was cleaning everything down that Maya told me about her afternoon trip with Easton. I dropped the spray and wipe, walked over to her, and sat before I pulled her onto my lap.

I folded my arms around her and asked, "You sure this is what you want? No one talked you into it?"

She shook her head. "Easton told me I didn't have to do this if I didn't want to."

"You feel you want to?"

Her hand ran up my chest. "Yes. I need to move forward. I need to make my choice, and this might help me do that."

"Okay, babe." I tucked some of her hair behind her ear and cupped the side of her neck. "Even if you don't pick, it doesn't matter."

"Texas, I'm wandering around, doing nothing with my life. I need a job."

"But you don't need to rush, and don't choose your old work because you're worried about your future. Be completely sure you want to go back, Maya. Can you do that? Because even if you don't go back, you'll find something else. There're other jobs out there."

She let out a soft sigh and nodded. "Okay."

I pulled her close and kissed her. Just a brief one. "Want me to come?"

She grinned. "Thank you for offering, but I'm not sure my boss will be happy if I showed up with my man. Easton I can get away with."

"All right, babe. Just know if you need me, I'll be there."

She melted into me, burying her face in my shoulder and neck. "You're being too sweet again."

Chuckling, I stood with her in my arms and then placed her on her feet. "I'll stop. Feed me, wench."

Her hands shot to her hips and her expression morphed into a pissed one. When I started laughing, she shoved me and stalked out. I followed her, not only because I knew there was food, but because I'd follow her anywhere.

When Easton arrived later, I pulled him aside while Maya was chatting with Parker who was driving them.

"I know you'll have her back, but watch for signs of her being overwhelmed."

Easton nodded. "I will."

"If she looks stressed, get her out."

He gave me a small smile. "I know, Texas."

"Don't let her boss talk her into anythin' out of guilt."

"I won't. I'll take care of her."

Nodding, I looked towards Maya, watching her laugh about something. I rubbed the back of my neck, feeling uneasy about her going. Was it too soon? Would she just jump back into working?

Easton's hand landed on my arm. "Don't worry. I've got her."

I tipped my chin up.

"You care for her, yeah?"

"She's mine."

His eyes widened. "Does she know?"

Some of the tension eased when I chuckled. "Yeah, she knows." Maya and Parker approached Easton from behind. "Don't you, babe?"

"Don't I what?" she asked, coming right at me to curl her arm around my waist, and I put mine around her back. Both Easton and Parker looked on with wide-eyed shock.

"You know you're mine, right?"

Maya blushed. "Not when you're annoying."

Parker snorted, swinging an arm around Easton's shoulders to tug him in close. "Isn't that always?"

Maya grinned. "He has his moments, but I'll let you know in a couple of months. This is only new."

"Talon know?" Parker asked, lips twitching.

"Yep. Already talked with him."

Maya squinted up at me. "I'd like to know what was said."

I tapped her nose. "Not gonna happen."

"This is cute," Easton announced. "I like it." He pressed a hand to Parker's gut. "Let me tell Lan."

Parker rolled his eyes. "Not like I was gonna ring him to gossip."

"Yes, you would have, and it wasn't like you had to drive us. You could have stayed at Stoke and Mally's with him."

"East" was all Parker said with a shake of his head. One of them was always with Easton when they weren't all together or Easton had work.

Easton rolled his eyes and glanced back at us. "Lucky you only have one to deal with, Maya."

I turned her into me so her front was plastered to my side. "Don't go givin' her any ideas, Easton. I don't share."

Parker chuckled while Easton grinned cheekily. "You don't know unless you try."

"No." I tugged Maya's head back and saw mirth in her gaze. "No one else but me, yeah?"

"Yes, Texas."

I grunted. "Good. Now kiss me and get goin'."

She got up onto her toes, pressed her lips to mine, and tried to pull back. I cupped the back of her head and kept her close.

"Come on, East," Parker said, and I heard them walk away.

Maya must have too, because she wrapped her arms around me and gave me what I wanted, a deep and heavy kiss that left me wanting more.

"You comin' back here after?"

"Is that okay?"

"Never ask that, babe." I kissed her nose. "I'll see you after."

"All right, Texas."

"Be safe and stick with what you're feelin' over work, yeah?"

"I will." She gave me a dazzling smile and left to meet Parker and Easton at their car. Parker shot me a chin lift, while Easton waved. I gave them a two-finger salute back.

They were good people and would take care of her.

Even knowing that, I watched until they drove off down the street, an uneasy feeling in my gut.

If she needed me, she'd call.

Maybe I should have told her that.

Shit, why didn't I say that?

I went to pull out my phone but stopped. No, she'd know she could call me about anything. She was coming here after it anyway, and then I could help her with whatever she'd decided.

Turning, I walked back inside.

"Who were those delicious specimens?" Mon asked. She'd told me a while ago that she and Hex liked to watch people. As in, they went to a certain type of club to watch other people get off while they got off together.

"Friends of ours."

"Friends? Is that all you're going to give me?"

I walked around the counter and started down the hall, ready to finish the design before Oliver showed.

"Texas," she whined.

Facing her, I smirked. "Mon, you don't have a chance to get them at the club. Parker won't let anyone watch Easton. Even if there was a miracle and he said yes, then you'd also have to go up against Lan, who's their third. He's just as protective of Easton as Parker."

"Oh hell, there's three?"

Snorting, I shook my head. "Not a chance, Mon."

She sighed. "Fine."

I went into the break room again to make myself a coffee and grab a muffin from what Maya had brought in. Fuck, she was sweet. In more ways than one. Grinning, I took my drink and food into my area and sat at my desk.

While I worked on Oliver's back piece, I couldn't help but wonder how Maya was going. I glanced at the clock.

They'd definitely be there. Was her boss already in her face, begging her to come back? Maya had a big heart. I worried she'd agree just to help out.

Groaning, I scrubbed a hand over my face and reached over to turn on my music. Turning it up louder, I got down to business. I'd soon see how it went, and then together, we'd deal with it.

CHAPTER TWENTY-FOUR

MAYA

As soon as I walked through the doors at the depot, I knew I'd made my choice. My throat closed over, my hands shook, and my heart beat frantically in my chest. Not only that, but tears formed as I took a step back.

Thank Christ for Easton. He curled me into him and eased me out of the depot.

I couldn't work here.

I didn't want to.

It was the last place I wanted to be.

Standing off to the side outside of the building, Easton helped me calm down, but every time the doors opened and the alarm sounded, I panicked.

Maybe one day I could go back to being a paramedic, but it wasn't now.

"Maya?"

Wiping at my face, I sucked in a shuddering breath and faced the voice I knew. My boss, Cassandra. "Hi, Cass."

Her bright smile faded. "Are you all right?"

I gave her a half shrug. "I am, but it's just...." Easton stood behind me with his hands on my shoulders. His support helped. "I'm not sure if I'll ever return, but for now, I know this job isn't for me."

She nodded, smiling gently. "I understand, Maya. But will you keep us as an option in a couple of years? You're a gifted paramedic, so don't rule us out forever."

"I won't, and please pass on my farewell to everyone. I'll try and come back another day."

"You got it." She reached out and gave my upper arm a squeeze. "Take care."

"I will, and you too."

When she was inside the building, I turned to Easton. "I'm sorry. I-I know what I went through doesn't justify this kind of anxiety—"

"Maya, no. Don't play off what happened to you. It was big, and even if it wasn't, it doesn't matter to anyone else how *you* deal with it. If you never want to be a paramedic again, who cares? It's what *you* want. What you can deal with. Don't worry about anyone else."

My smile was a little crooked, and even I knew it wasn't all there—my emotions were too raw. I hadn't expected to react this way. I thought I'd at least get in there to see people, to say thank you for their support, but I couldn't even do that.

"Come on. Let's get out of here," Easton said gently and curled his arm around my shoulders to lead me towards the car.

"You can go in. Please don't let me stop you."

"Honey, I'll be honest. I had a feeling you would make up your mind if you came here. I'm not sure if I've done the right thing by pushing you, but I didn't want you to deal with the anxiety of not making a choice."

I stopped. Easton did too.

"Maya?"

I had been putting off making a choice, but finally knowing I didn't want to work here was like a weight had been swept free from my shoulders. Clarity set in. Being a paramedic wasn't for me at this time, but it wasn't off the cards altogether. I was only twenty-one and had a lot more living to do yet. Who knew where my future would lead me?

"Did I do the wrong thing?" Easton asked before he bit down on his bottom lip.

I threw my arms around his waist. "Thank you."

"What?" he uttered, confusion in his tone.

Pulling back, I gave him an affectionate smile. "I've been in limbo. Sitting on the fence about this for so long. With you bringing me here, I can move on. Move forward."

He exhaled loudly. "Oh, thank God. I thought I messed up big time and Texas was going to kick my butt."

A snort sounded from behind him. "Not that I'd let it happen."

Easton turned to Parker. "What are you doing out of the car?"

"Babe, I ain't a dog. I can get out of the car on my own. I worried Maya was stranglin' you."

Laughing, I linked my arm through Easton's, and together we walked to Parker and then the car.

Easton opened the door to the back seat for me. But before I got in, he took my wrist. "Are you sure you're okay?"

Nodding, I hugged him tightly. "I'm the best I have been in a long time." Not only did I have an answer, but I had Texas in my life... just the way I wanted him.

ONCE I'D REASSURED Texas I was good after going to the depot, I took Easton and Parker to his place for a coffee, which I was sure also helped reassure Texas I was okay.

As we drank and chatted, I realised it was good to catch up with them. Even though they came to family barbeques at the compound, sometimes they couldn't make it, while other times there wasn't enough hours at the family event to see everyone there. To say our family was big was a huge understatement.

"How's the tribe of dogs?"

Easton had the biggest heart and rescued dogs; he had about six of them the last time I heard.

Parker's hand went from Easton's thigh to wrap his arm around his lover's shoulders.

Shit.

Easton's lips thinned. He tried to tip them up but failed. "We lost two recently. Old age. It happens."

"But it still hurts all the same."

He nodded. "It does." He took a breath and changed the subject, which I understood. "So, have you and Texas moved in together?"

My cheeks heated as I laughed awkwardly. "No. It's way too soon for that. We only started officially dating two days ago, or was it yesterday?" I shrugged. "One of those."

Their brows shot high.

I shifted nervously on the seat. "Is it bad that I'm here at his house without him when we've only just started dating?"

Easton waved a hand in front of him. "No, no. It's not that. We just thought it had been longer."

"Oh yeah?"

They nodded.

"Well, it hasn't. We might act closer than other couples starting out, but it's because we've been in each other's lives for ages. I had the biggest crush on him when I was younger and got annoyed when he would bring women around in front of me. Which made me avoid him for a long time because it broke my heart. But then we grew closer after what happened, and since then, we've been inseparable."

Easton grabbed Parker's hand in both of his. "That's so sweet."

"He's got a good woman," Parker added.

I shrugged and threw out a hand, not knowing what to say, which both of them got a laugh out of.

Parker's phone chimed, and he pulled it out. "Lan's ready. We better head off." They stood up, and I followed them to the door, thanking Easton once again. With a hug from both, they asked me to say goodbye to Texas and mentioned we should go to Melton for lunch one day, which I agreed to. Then they were gone, and I suddenly didn't know what to do with myself.

Did I go back to Texas's shop? But he was probably busy with a client.

Would it be imposing if I tidied a little? He was at work, and I had nothing to do. I wouldn't want to come home to a messy house. Not that it wasn't clean. But I did spot some dirty laundry. Maybe washing his clothes went too far and too soon.

Was I supposed to go home? But then I remembered that Texas said he wanted to see me tonight.

Groaning, I went into the kitchen where my bag sat on the counter and pulled out my phone. I unlocked it and pressed on Mum's number.

"Sweetie, where are you?"

"At Texas's."

Silence.

"Mum?"

"Tell me everything," she demanded in a quiet whisper.

She was my mum. We'd always been close. Of course I told her everything, except for the details of what happened in the bedroom.

"Oh my God. *Oh my God*. Oh, sweetie, that sounds like a dream. He really said all of that?"

"Yes."

"Are you happy?" she asked softly.

"Yes. It's a rush, but... everything to me."

"You deserve this. Both of you do. And, Maya, don't you worry about it being so soon. It's not really. You've known each other a long time. You've been half in love with him since you were sixteen, and I knew that when that boy caught feelings, they would stick."

"So, it's not weird I'm here in his house without him?"

"What? No, don't be silly."

"It's just... all of it will take me a little to get used to, but then again, it won't. Do you know what I mean?"

"I definitely do."

"Oh, uh, I also went to work with Easton and came to a decision. I-I...." I blew out a breath, suddenly a little apprehensive because my parents had helped me with my course expenses.

"Maya, no matter what your decision is, we'll stand by you. You have nothing to worry about either way."

It really was silly of me to get worried about telling Mum. "For now, I'm not going back."

"Okay, sweetie. I'm so happy you know what you want. Your dad and I are always here, you know this. For anything."

"I know, Mum."

"Good—wait one second, Maya. Someone's at the door." I heard her open it. "Texas? What are you doing here?"

I stilled, even my breath.

"Came to grab an overnight bag for Maya, if that's all right?"

Oh. My. God. I sucked in a breath and pressed a hand to my belly. And here I was worried about doing some housework. I wouldn't anymore.

My body warmed and my heart expanded with all the mushy feelings.

"Of course," Mum said, and I could hear the smile in her voice. "I'll go and get some things together."

"Mum, tell him I'll see him soon, and to you, I'll be home tomorrow. We'll catch up more then."

"I will, sweetie. Bye."

With a silly laugh, I spun, clutching my phone to my chest. Texas made me feel like I was a lovesick actress from a movie. I would do anything to hold on to the way he made me feel.

By the time he got back, it was nearly dinnertime, and I already had a stir-fry ready from the ingredients in his refrigerator. When I heard the back door sliding open, I jolted a little, and a jumble of nerves hit my stomach.

I turned and smiled shyly.

"Babe," he said as he dropped a bag inside the door and came at me. He swept me up in his arms, causing me to gasp and then laugh. "Fuck, it's good to see you here when I walk in."

"Hey." I smiled warmly.

He grinned. "Hey. You gonna kiss your man or do I have to—"

I curled my arms around his neck and kissed him with a brush of lips once, twice, and on the third, I slanted my mouth over his and opened up to him.

When we parted, both of us were out of breath.

"That's how I want you to kiss me every time we've been apart and come together again."

"Okay, Texas," I said softly.

He rearranged me to curl my front into his side. "What did you make?"

"Just a simple stir-fry."

"Smells fuckin' amazin'. Can you turn it down or off? We'll shower and then eat."

Grinning with mirth, I patted his chest. "Is showering together all you've thought about all day?"

"Most of the day, yeah."

Shaking my head, I lightly laughed, even when my

belly fluttered over the thought of being naked in the shower with Texas. "Then let's go shower." I reached out to turn off the stovetop.

CHAPTER TWENTY-FIVE

TEXAS

A squeal escaped Maya when I took her in my arms and flipped her around before bending to pick her up over my shoulder. I strode down the hall and into my bedroom with a laughing woman. Her humour died when I entered the bathroom, helped her stand, and pulled my tee over my head.

"Undress, gorgeous," I ordered and moved over to turn on the shower. Adjusting the water, I glanced over my shoulder to see Maya slipping her jeans and panties down her legs. She straightened, only wearing her black top, and I couldn't help but think she'd look fucking spectacular in nothing but one of my tees.

Scraping my top teeth over my bottom lip, I shifted back to fix the water temp one last time as my cock throbbed hard. I sucked in a sharp breath when the soft heat of Maya's tits pushed into my back as she wrapped her arms around my waist. My dick damn near fought to get out of my jeans.

She pressed a kiss between my shoulder blades.

"Step back, babe," I said, gruffer than usual, but shit, the desire for my woman was pumping through me. When she did, I faced her fully, taking her in. She was goddamn stunning. I quickly undid my jeans, pushed them and my boxers down while I kicked off my shoes, and then took off my socks. My cock ached, hard and ready.

Finally naked, I picked my woman up and walked us under the spray of water, taking her mouth in a hard kiss she opened up to right away.

As I ran my mouth down her neck, I felt her tiny laugh and lifted my face. "What?"

"I could get used to showers with you."

Grinning, I grunted and tipped my chin up. "Good. Now let me get my hands on your hair to wash it."

"You want to wash my hair?"

"Babe. I fuckin' love your hair, so yeah, I wanna wash it."

My heart expanded when I saw the warmth in her eyes. She nodded and turned, taking the shampoo from its holder and passing it back to me. After I shampooed and conditioned hers, I quickly washed mine, since all it needed was a shampoo.

I brushed the water from my eyes and opened them to see Maya's wide ones. "You only shampoo?"

"Yeah. It's all it needs."

"But I've felt your hair. It's always soft."

"I know."

"Are you saying you *only* shampoo and it's always that soft?"

Chuckling, I nodded. "Yeah."

She planted her hands on her hips, glaring. "You lucky SOB."

I swiped water from my face again and grinned. "Are you gettin' pissed 'cause I only have to use shampoo?"

"Yes! You don't know what a pain it is taking care of this"—she waved to her head—"to keep it nice and soft. After this shower, I'll have to put leave-in conditioner in it, *and* I'll still have to use some type of product in the morning."

"Babe," I started, tugging her close with my arm around her waist. "You really want to talk about hair, or you wanna put your hands on the wall so I can play with your pussy?"

Her gaze went hazy. "Oh... um, option two, please."

Smirking, I shook my head, wanting to laugh. "All right, then do it."

When she didn't move at first, I helped her by planting my hands on her waist and turning her. Her breaths became little pants when I ran my hands from her waist to her wrists so I could lift her arms. When she slapped her hands onto the tiles, I brushed her hair from one shoulder to kiss her there.

"My Maya, beautiful, sweet, and willin' to please her man." She shivered from my words spoken close to her ear. I sucked her lobe into my mouth while gliding a hand down her back to her arse.

"Texas," she whimpered.

"Soon, gorgeous," I told her, rubbing my hard-as-fuck cock into her hip.

She gasped when I slapped her arse cheek hard. Her head dropped back, eyes closed, mouth open. I rubbed over the sting while I wrapped my other hand around her neck and lightly tightened my hold. Her eyes flashed open, but I didn't see concern. I saw pure fucking arousal.

I gripped her throat harder and slapped her arse again. She choked out a moan.

"Fuck, babe. You're so good for me. You liked that, didn't you?"

I squeezed her neck once again. Her face turned red, and when I let go, she heaved her breaths in and out.

"Yes."

"Yes what, Maya?"

"I liked it."

Christ, I was giving her all I enjoyed, and she got off on it. She seriously was made for me.

"Hell, babe. Bet you're drenched for me." I removed my hand from her neck and cupped it over her pussy. "So soaked, it's leakin' from you."

She whimpered, dropping her head and trying to rock down on my hand.

"Not yet, gorgeous."

"Texas," she complained. "Please," she begged.

Fuck yes.

"Turn. Press your back to the tiles," I ordered.

She did, letting out a gasp at the coolness touching her flushed skin. She licked her lips, looking up at me.

Goddamn stunning.

My cock throbbed, fucking *ached* at the sight of her. The way her chest rose and fell rapidly, pushing her tits up and down. Bending, I licked at her left nipple but kept my eyes on her. Watching when her lips parted. Her pupils widened as I bit and sucked.

I ran my hands down her sides, over her hips, and slipped one between her legs where I had her spread them more. I straightened to cover her throat again with my large, tatted hand while using the other to shove two fingers inside her. She went onto her toes and cried my name. I curled the fingers up and rubbed as I applied pressure to her neck.

"Texas," she breathed, slamming her eyes closed, biting her bottom lip and whimpering as I fucked her with my fingers and pressed my thumb to her clit.

"That's it, babe. Fuck, you look beautiful... full with my fingers and red from my hand." I let go of her neck, and she gasped her breaths. I kissed her hard, and she moaned into my mouth.

Pushing my fingers deeper, I trailed kisses down her

neck, over her shoulder, and when I got to the top of her tit, I bit down. She cried out. The squelching from her drenched-as-fuck pussy had my dick throbbing over and over. I knew it wouldn't take me long to come, but I wouldn't until I'd taken care of my woman.

I kissed my way back up while finger-fucking her to the point that her legs started to shake.

"Texas, God, please."

"Right here, babe. Christ, you feel good. So wet, so tight, and now marked by me. Gonna mark you more. Gonna come all over you, rub it into your skin. Make you mine."

Her hand tightened around my arm. She gaped, closing her eyes, and I nipped at her bottom lip.

"Texas," she yelled before I kissed her through her orgasm.

Her body shook, and if I thought she was wet before, it was nothing like the gush she'd produced at climax.

Hell, it was the hottest things I'd seen and felt.

When she'd come down, I withdrew my fingers and wrapped my hand around my cock. I used my other hand to cup the back of her head and tilt it down. "Watch me come on you, Maya. Fuckin' watch what you do to me. I ain't gonna last. You drive me wild, babe."

Her arm curled around my waist as I tucked her close and eyed her as she looked at my hand pumping my dick fast.

"Christ," I grunted through teeth, exploding my load over her gut, pussy, and legs. When I kept coming, I buried my face into her neck, groaning through it, and finally slumping when I was spent.

IT WAS LATER, after we'd dried off and eaten dinner, that we sat on the couch to watch some TV, and I pulled Maya from beside me onto my lap.

"Wanna make sure, babe, that you're cool with your decision about work?"

She smiled, tucking herself close, but facing me more. "I am. Completely. I don't know what I'll do for work, but for right now, it's not being a paramedic."

"Glad you got that sorted in your head, gorgeous. I can help with the job if you want."

She laughed. "What, are you going to give me one? Not sure I can tattoo as good as you, baby."

Smirking, I shook my head. "You're forgettin' Mon's gonna have her own room soon, and I'll need a girl out the front."

She stilled, gaze widening. "I can't work for you."

I jerked my head back. "Why the fuck not?"

"We're together."

"And?"

"I can't sleep with the boss."

Christ. I dropped my head back and laughed my arse

off. I pulled her close, or at least tried to, but she pushed at my chest.

"Quit laughing."

"No, babe, that shit was funny."

"How?"

"You can't be serious about not taking the job because I'd be your boss and we're together."

"Um, yeah. People will think I'm abusing the relationship and falling into an easy job."

I gave her a squeeze. "Quiet," I clipped. "I don't give a fuck what people think. You reckon you could do the job?"

She licked her lips, glanced away and back again. "Well, yes."

"Then the job's yours. I've interviewed a fuckin' billion people, and none of them fit. You do, and Christ, it's a bonus that I get to see you whenever the fuck I want."

"But what happens if spending too much time together ruins us?"

"It won't."

"Texas, I'm serious."

"Right, if you think it's too much, we'll talk it out when the time comes."

"Oh, um, okay."

"So, you gonna take the job?"

"Yes... I think so. But if I do, I won't stay here all the time. We'll need some time away from each other or I'll drive you insane. Then again, you could send me over the edge too."

"Babe," I bit out. "Do your 'rents take timeouts? I know Dodge and Low don't, and *they* work and live together."

"They're married, Texas."

I lifted her so she straddled my lap. "And this between us, where's it goin'? Are you only with me for a short time?"

"No, but—"

"Don't want to hear any buts, Maya. Let's ride this out together and see how it goes. If you need a night away, go to your 'rents. If you don't, stay here."

"You'll tell me if you need time alone?"

"I won't want time alone, but fine."

"Texas," she whispered, getting in my face and cupping my cheeks. Hell, I wanted to laugh, but I didn't. "We've only started dating and you're talking about... well, it sounds a lot like me just living with you."

I thought about it for a second and realised it really did.

Then I shrugged. "So?"

She groaned, dropping her hands from my face to thump her forehead on my shoulder near my neck. "You're insane."

"Don't believe I am, babe. How about we just take each day as it comes? Like I said, if you stay here the night after working with me all day, it'd be good. If you don't, I'll still see you at work." However, I had a very strong feeling she would be in my bed each and every night. There was a high chance I'd drag her there.

She'd eventually understand that I'd got her words clearly when she told me she'd been into me since she was sixteen. I didn't care if I was late into the play and only been in love with her for over half a year.

All that mattered was that she was mine and I was hers.

I rocked my legs up, jostling her. "Yeah, Maya?"

She lifted her head and drew in an unsteady breath, but she nodded, and my fucking heart swelled when she said, "Okay, Texas."

Grinning, I cupped the side of her neck. "Good. Now, I gotta check on somethin' else." She looked wary but waited me out. "I need to make sure you enjoyed our play in the shower. Don't want you thinkin' I was too rough with you or anythin'."

Her cheeks burned with a blush. "Texas." She shook her head.

"Need to know, babe."

Sighing, she looked away and said, "I liked it. Um..." She licked her lips and the blush spread. "You weren't too rough. You could, ah, go further."

Fucking shit.

My spent cock tried to perk up.

I threaded my fingers through her hair and pulled her close. "Glad to know, babe. We'll definitely fuckin' explore that."

"Okay," she breathed against my lips before I took her mouth in a hungry kiss.

CHAPTER TWENTY-SIX

MAYA

"*B*abe." Texas pressed a kiss to my shoulder. I groaned and slapped a hand back to push at him. He chuckled. "Told you not to have that last shot."

Like a child, and since I was on the verge of losing my stomach, I mimicked his voice, "Told you not to have that last shot." I took a breath and ignored his chuckle. "Texas. I love you, but now's not the time to be a smartarse."

I froze. I hadn't meant to say that, and it was definitely too soon. We'd only been together a few weeks now. Though I'd loved him long before that.

He grabbed my shoulder and rolled me onto my back. My belly churned.

"What did you say?" he clipped, but his eyes said a lot more. They were lit with a heat I hadn't seen before.

"Now's not the time to be a smartarse?" I tried.

He shook his head. "No, not that."

His hand slipped to my throat and applied a little pressure. "Babe, tell me."

"It's too soon," I muttered, my heart galloping behind my ribs.

"Says who?"

I didn't have an answer for that, and by the smug look on Texas's face, he knew it.

"No one's gonna hear it but me. Unless you didn't mean it."

I glared and shoved his shoulder. "You *know*."

His lips twitched. "Know what?"

"Texas Monroe, don't play games with me."

"Then tell me."

Sighing, I looked off to the side, rolled my eyes, and then looked back at the man who meant the world to me. Searching his face, I stopped on his gaze, and whispered, "I love you, Texas."

His grin took my breath away. He dipped down to press his lips to mine. Against them, he said, "Fuck, babe. I love you too." His hand tightened, drawing out a gasp. He pulled his head back a little. "You're everything to me, and I'm never lettin' you go, so don't go gettin' any ideas of gettin' away from me. I will hunt you."

"Baby, if I wasn't on the verge of throwing up, I would jump you right now."

He threw his head back and laughed. God, he was handsome.

When he was done, he kissed the corner of my mouth. "I gotta get a shower in before the client shows. You get over this hangover, and later I'm fuckin' you hard."

"Sounds good to me."

He climbed off the bed.

"And you know it's your fault I got drunk."

"Babe" was all he said with a smirk before he went into the en suite. He might not have thought the blame should go to him, but it wasn't me who started with the drinking at the compound in the first place.

"Maya," he called, poking his head out the door. "Do you remember the drive home?"

I scrunched my nose in thought and then it hit me.

"Oh God," I groaned.

I wanted to slap his wide grin off his face. He winked and disappeared, then I heard the shower turning on.

We'd rode Texas's bike over to the compound to catch up with whoever was there. It wasn't until I was sloshed that Dad and Mum showed and offered to drive us home.

Texas got me into the back of their car behind the driver's seat, and I leaned forward, nearly strangling Dad as I hugged him.

"I love you guys so, so much."

"Sweetie, are you trying to kill your father?" Mum tapped my arm.

"Oops." I laughed and let go. I'd scooted into the middle

seat when Texas got in the other side. "Do you know what I said the other day?"

"What?" Dad asked, rubbing at his throat.

"I told Texas how perfect my parents are. Didn't I?" I reached back and slapped Texas on the chest. But then I got distracted by the hardness and turned in my seat to look at him. "Have I told you how hot you are today?"

From the front seats, someone groaned as if in pain. But Texas's face was important.

Texas chuckled. "Not today, but now you have."

"Good." I nodded. "I like when you—"

"Maya!" Talon growled.

I jumped and faced the front of the car. "Hey, I'm here. I have the best parents. Mum, why you laughing? Wait—doesn't matter, because I remember that you, Dad, you didn't even get pissed when I didn't come home for ages."

"You still haven't been home," Dad pointed out.

"Are you sure?" I asked. "Wait, I was there the other day."

"For dinner after you'd taken Ruby and Drake to your place."

"Hmm. I have the best siblings. I should ring them." I searched my pockets, but I couldn't find my phone.

"Maya, maybe now's not a good time to call them," Mum suggested.

"What? Why?"

"Babe, come here and buckle in so we can get home."

"Home. I like that. Home." I scooted back, and Texas

helped me get my seat belt on because it was suddenly diffi-cult. "Mum!" I yelled.

"Jesus," Dad cursed.

"Yes, Maya?"

"I think I'm living with Texas."

She giggled. "I think you are too."

"You guys are the best. Dad, thanks for not killing him."

He snorted. "You're welcome."

"Okay. I'm just gonna have a little sleep."

Then I'd passed out. I didn't even remember getting to bed. God, my parents were going to give me hell, and they'd probably told everyone about it. In our family, embarrassing situations always spread like wildfire.

Groaning again, I rolled onto my side as I heard the shower switch off. I closed my eyes for a moment and compelled my stomach to stop rolling. I needed to get up and take some Panadol. I could also drink a gallon of water.

"Babe" was said softly.

I opened my eyes, and my heart skipped a beat. He'd read my mind.

"You're amazing," I told him, sitting. I took the medicine and gulped down the water. "Promise I'll be into work soon."

"Don't stress. Just whenever, or not at all. See how you go."

I cocked a brow. "Is this because I sleep with the boss?"

He grinned. "That and I don't want you chuckin' in

the shop. Hex has a weak stomach, and Mon will just bitch."

Smiling, I nodded, and slipped back down. "Just need five."

He leaned over and pressed his mouth to mine. "Love you."

My whole body warmed. "Love you too," I answered, blinking the sudden tears away.

His grin turned into a gentle smile as he wiped them from my face. With a wink, he bopped me on the nose and left.

I'd hit the jackpot with this guy. I still wasn't sure what I'd done for him to finally notice me, but I would be forever grateful. And for the sweet actions he'd shown after the attack.

Closing my eyes, I thought I'd rest just for a moment longer. But when I opened them again, I knew more time had gone by. On the plus side, I felt better.

Then I remembered Texas telling me he loved me, and my pulse raced.

When I showered, his words swept through my mind again, and I couldn't stop smiling.

As I made some sandwiches for everyone next door, it slipped into my mind again. My belly fluttered and I went to the shop, feeling a million times better than I had when he'd woke me earlier.

The bell above the door rang when I entered, and I called out, "It's just me."

Mon appeared from her room. "I heard someone has a hangover."

Rolling my eyes, I said loudly, "And *someone* has a big mouth."

"You love it," we heard yelled back from Texas's room and then chuckles followed.

"Are you on a break?" I asked Mon while ignoring the rest.

"I was just going to head out and grab something to eat."

I held up the basket. "I made things. Can you take it into the lunchroom? I've already eaten."

"You got it, and thanks, Maya, *you're the best*," she cooed, and I glared towards Texas's room, knowing he'd talked about the trip home with my parents.

Just as I got behind the counter, the front door opened, and I looked up to smile wide.

"My precious buttercup, how you doing?" Julian, my uncle who was married to Mum's brother, walked in with his hips swaying.

"Julian, what are you doing here?"

"I'm peeved I missed the fun last night, so I wanted to drop by to invite you and Texas over for cocktails next Friday night."

"If I stop feeling sick by then, we'd love to."

He stopped by the counter and leaned his hip against it. "Shouldn't you ask Texas first?"

"No, he'll come." I smiled.

"Aww, this is so adorable. Do you think we could get Texas so drunk that he'll take his clothes off?"

"Julian!"

He tried for an innocent look. "What? You can't be the only one who gets to look at all his tattoos."

"And I'm sure you just want to look at his tats."

He leaned in. "Come on, you can tell your favourite uncle. How *big* is he?"

Laughing, I palmed his face and pushed him back. "I'm not saying anything."

Julian grinned. "We'll see how it goes Friday, then. Anyway, I must be off. I have to get home to pick up Aelia. She's going to the movies with her friends, but there's boys going as well."

"Will it be you or Mattie hiding in the theatre?"

He winked. "Mattie. Apparently, he doesn't trust me enough to be quiet."

Snorting, I nodded. "I agree with him."

"You're an evil child. Though, I suppose you're not a child now since you're riding on the Texas train."

Groaning, I ran a hand over my face. "Oh my God, Julian."

He blew me a kiss and headed for the door. "Tootles." Then he was gone, but it only lasted about five minutes before he was opening the door again.

"Did you forget something?" I asked.

He came in, lips thin, and stepped aside. "This young lady was asking me if Texas works here."

The woman seemed a few years older than me. She

was tall and slim with long black hair and green eyes. She was very attractive, and the jean shorts and tank top she wore clung to her like a second skin.

I smiled, thinking she was an old client from Melbourne. "Hi, Texas does work here. But he's with a client right now. Did you want me to pass on a message?"

She looked me up and down with her nose raised. My brows dipped, wondering what I'd done to cause her judgy face. I glanced at Julian who shrugged.

"Go and tell him Jules is here."

"Sorry, but he doesn't like to be interrupted."

She glared. "I know what he likes and doesn't. Just do your job."

A door opened down the hall, and I prayed it was Hex or Mon. We all glanced that way, and I clenched my teeth when Texas's client appeared. If Texas was done, he'd come looking for me.

"Hi, Jerry. All done?"

"Sure am." Jerry showed off his forearm.

I beamed. "Looks amazing."

"I know. Texas knows what he's doing."

The woman suddenly said, "So he's done. Good, then go get him."

Jerry turned to this bitch, checked her out, and then turned back to me. "Can I fix my account?"

"You sure can. Give me one second to fire up the computer." I moved that way and gave Julian big eyes. He returned the look.

"Honey, can I ask why you want to see Texas?" Julian asked Jules.

"None of your damn business, gaybo."

She did not.

She. Did. Not.

"Excuse me a moment, Jerry." I smiled and then slapped my palm to the counter. "You." I pointed at the woman. "How dare you come in here and disrespect people." I wanted to rip her hair out and throat punch her.

"Just get me Texas—"

"Jules? What the fuck are you doin' here?"

Her sour face changed in seconds. She smiled and flicked her hair over her shoulder. "Texas. It's so good to see you."

"Not sure why you're here, but you need to leave," he clipped as he came to stand beside me, crossing his arms over his chest.

"Texas, don't be silly. Cal and I broke up. I knew you'd want to know. How about we go get a drink somewhere?"

Crossing *my* arms over my chest, I glared up at Texas. "Do you want to explain something to me?"

"Ooooh, I popped in at the right time," I heard Julian say.

"Babe, her boyfriend Cal was my client in Melbourne. She used to come with him all the time. I didn't know she wanted something off me."

"She wants to ride the Texas train too."

We all shot our glares to Julian, who mimicked zipping his lips.

Sighing, I turned to Jules. "I'm sorry you came all this way, but Texas is actually dating someone." I thumbed at my chest.

She snorted. "Texas doesn't date. I just want to try what all my girls have been talking about."

"Fuck," Texas bit out.

Reaching out, I smacked Texas in the stomach. "Texas, *baby*, I can't hurt you for your past, but you need to fix this and set her straight before I lose my cool."

My man's lips twitched as he curled an arm around my shoulders and brought me in close, kissing the top of my head. "Jules, those days are gone for me, and I'm glad for it. My future is standin' right here." He shook me a little. "I'm completely committed to my woman."

Jules placed her hands on her hips. "Are you serious?"

His face went cold. "Deadly."

She clenched her jaw, huffed, and then turned, walking out the already open door where Julian still stood.

"Thank you for the entertainment," Julian called. "Texas, I'll see you Friday. Maya, smooches."

When he was gone, Texas looked down at me. "What's happenin' Friday?"

"Dinner and drinks at Julian and Mattie's place."

"Jesus. You'll owe me."

I scoffed. "I think, after that sweet little visit, it's you who owes me."

"Ah, can I pay my bill now?" Jerry asked.

"Shit, Jerry, I'm so sorry you had to see that." I went to walk back to the computer when I was tagged around the waist, spun, and kissed senseless.

Texas pulled back, and I blinked slowly up at him. "Love you, babe."

"Love you too, but you still owe me."

Chuckling, he swatted my butt and went back down the hall. After Jerry paid and left, I still found myself smiling because it didn't matter about Texas and his past. I'd seen it firsthand back in the day, and honestly, it didn't surprise me something like this would pop up. Texas had a fan group, no doubt. If it did happen again, I would deal with that too. Texas was mine, and with his eyes now wide open, all he saw was me.

EPILOGUE

MAYA

"*H*ow you doin', babe?"

"Shut up." I hissed out a breath when he hit a very sensitive spot. I swear if I heard him chuckle one more time, I was going to rip his balls off. "How in the hell have you done this, like, a trillion times?"

He paused to shrug. "I like the feelin'."

"You're crazy," I told him and then hissed again when he started back up. I glanced down between my breasts at the sternum tattoo Texas was doing.

"Babe, I told you this spot was one of the most painful ones."

"I know," I cried. "I should have listened, but it'll look badarse when it's done."

"It will, gorgeous, and you've done so fuckin' well. It's nearly finished. The outlining is the worst."

Right, I could do this. It'd already been an hour. What was a little longer? Besides, as soon as I'd seen Texas drawing the hawk one night when we'd been sitting on the couch together, I knew it was perfect for me. It represented so much. Not only for my dad and his club, but the way Texas had the wings spread under my breasts, to me, stood for my freedom from living through a terrible event. I also liked to think it was for my future. One Texas and I were flying into together.

I scraped my top teeth over my bottom lip and winced. "I would watch you more if my face wasn't screwed up. I love seeing you work."

I felt his lips press against the side of my boob.

"I know, babe."

"You won't tell anyone I was a mess, right?"

"My lips are sealed."

"Promise me, Texas, because you didn't keep your mouth shut about the time when the spider attacked me or the many other times over the year we've been together when I've done something you've found hilarious."

I opened my eyes to catch him grinning.

"Babe, I promise to keep my mouth shut about this. Those things were different. They were funny. Your pain isn't."

God, that was sweet.

"Thank you, baby."

"Always. Now, quit movin'. I'm nearly done."

LILA ROSE

Nodding, I closed my eyes and gripped the sides of the
bed. The gun buzzed to life, and I gritted my teeth
through the rest, since there was no way I would tap out. I
wanted this tattoo. Maybe next time, if there was going to
be one, I would stick to places on my body that wouldn't
take my breath away or have me in near tears.

I still couldn't believe it had been a year today since we
got together. I wouldn't change a thing. We had our little
spats about silly things, but we'd stuck together no matter
how much we got on each other's nerves.

Things hadn't really changed for us. We worked and
went home together. Went to the compound to hang out
and drink. Sometimes Texas had things he needed to do
with the brothers. Situations where I didn't know what he
would be walking into. Mum told me the worry never got
old. She still feared for Dad every time something
happened and the club had to step in to assist. Really, we'd
been lucky there hadn't been anything big where they had
to go in guns blazing. Though even the smaller incidents
were scary.

But this was our life. The club would always be a part
of it, and I'd already accepted that even before Texas and I
got together, courtesy of growing up in a club.

Which was why we loved hard and enjoyed life to the
fullest.

When my phone chimed, I glanced to the side where it
was on the bench.

"It's Swan," Texas told me after he took a glance.

"Can I grab it?"

He stopped tattooing long enough for me to grab my phone, unlock it, and open the message.

SWAN:

> He's coming back to Australia.

ME:

Who?

SWAN:

> Lockland!!!!

ME:

OMG. When, where, why?

SWAN:

> For concerts, and he's coming back in a couple of years, but the report says he's thinking of staying a while. Should I reach out?

She was panicking already, but it wouldn't happen for a couple of years? Honestly, her nerves said a lot about this guy. He'd been such a great friend to Swan back in the day, and I'd always hoped for more for both of them, but then he'd up and moved. I was sure I hadn't been the only one hoping for more between the two of them. Not that Swan would openly admit that.

ME:

> Do you want to?

"What's happenin'?" Texas asked, and I told him. He didn't really remember Lockland, so he didn't understand how big this was. He rolled his eyes, smirked, and got back to work while I held my phone high.

SWAN:

> I don't know. He's the one who stopped talking to me.

And it had broken her heart. I even tried to reach out to him to see what was happening, but he never returned my texts or calls. I could handle not hearing from him, since we hadn't been close, but for him to cut ties with Swan, I didn't understand. He'd always thought the world of her. Unless maybe he'd moved on and found someone who didn't like their connection, or, and I hated to think it, fame had gotten to his head, and he just didn't want anything to do with Swan now.

ME:

> How about when the time comes, we get tickets to his concert?

SWAN:

> I can't do that! I can't just show up at a concert.

ME:

Swan, you love his music, and there'll
be like a million other people there. It's
not like he'll see you... until you want
him to.

SWAN:

I'll think about it, but I've got to go.
Class.

ME:

Talk soon.

My super quiet and shy friend could use a little helping hand. I'd get some tickets just in case she wanted to go. I quickly checked the information about his return and noticed tickets wouldn't go on sale until it was confirmed and locked in next year. I put a reminder on my phone in my calendar for March the following year.

Texas turned off the machine and wiped over my tattoo. "All done, babe."

"Yay." He took my phone and put it down before helping me stand up so I could see it in the long mirror. "By the way, we'll be going to Lockland's concert in a couple of years."

"What's he sing?"

"A bit of everything, really."

He chuckled. "That doesn't give me much. I'll listen to some before I commit."

With my hands covering my breasts, I stopped in front

of the mirror and gasped. Tears welled and I bit down on my bottom lip.

I took a step closer as Texas moved in behind me, looking over my shoulder. He placed his hands on my hips. "Do you like it?"

"Baby, I love it," I whispered. His hands fell away when I moved even closer to twist from left to right.

Only to still.

I stepped closer again.

There, on the wing, I was sure I saw some writing.

I wasn't imagining it.

I couldn't be.

Blinking, I leaned in. It took me a little while to read the words in my head since they were backwards. *Love you always and forever. Will you marry me?*

"Baby," I whispered. My eyes welled. I blinked slowly again as the tears fell and kept staring at it. "Texas," I muttered, my voice tight.

Slowly, I turned and rocked back, eyes and mouth wide.

Texas was down on one knee.

"Maya Marcus, there is no one else for me because you're all I want in my future forever. You're my heart-beat, my pulse, and my soul. I can't imagine a day without you, and life is too short to wait any longer to make you mine. Will you marry me?"

I covered my face with my hands and burst into tears. Arms circled me, warmth seeped into me, and lips pressed against my head, my cheek, and my temple.

"Maya, babe?"

Sniffing, I wiped roughly at my face and looked up at my man. Gripping his waist, I nodded. "Yes, Texas. It would be an honour to marry you."

"Thank fuck," he breathed, and it had me laughing. Texas shifted back and slid the beautiful diamond ring onto my finger. He kissed the back of it, tucked some of my hair behind my ear, and then kissed me until I was dizzy.

Breaking from me, he pulled me over to the table. "Glad you like the tat, babe."

"I more than like it. I love it."

"Worth the pain?" he asked as he grabbed my tee.

"Yes."

"Good."

I drew my brows down when he pushed the tee over my head. I thought he'd taken me to the table for a different reason, not to dress me.

"What's going on?"

"Nothin'." He took my hand and dragged me out of the room.

"Don't you need to clean it?"

"Later."

"But..." I glanced back at the room. "I thought we were going to have sex to celebrate."

He grunted, dropped his head, but then lifted my hand with the ring on it. I was too busy looking up at my hand in the air to notice.

Until the room erupted into cheers.

I startled and looked at our families in the reception area of the shop.

Mum, Dad, Cody, Channa, Drake, and Ruby. Plus, Julian and Mattie with Aelia. Even Aunt Violet, Travis, and Izzy were there. As well as Low, Dodge, and Rommy.

Mum, Low, and Julian were crying. Dad, Dodge, and Uncle Mattie were consoling the ones crying happy tears with eye rolls or sighs. The rest were smiling big.

"I could have done without knowin' you wanted to get naked, sis," Drake said, since he was the first to approach.

"Oh God, please forget that."

"Don't worry, I will. I'm bleaching my brain later. Congrats, you guys." He grinned, hugging us. The others all came forward and congratulated Texas and me.

"Party at Texas's," Low yelled, and people started filing out.

Dad stayed, though. He stood in front of Texas and me with thin lips and hard eyes. Until they softened when he cupped my cheeks. "You'll always be my little girl. No matter what, you know you can come to us if he pisses you off, and I'll kill him."

Sniffing, I blinked the tears out, and said, "I know, Dad."

I gripped Texas's hand tightly when I saw Dad's jaw clenched. "You've grown up into an amazing woman, Maya. I'm proud of you."

"Dad," I choked, emotions clogging me.

"Love you, darlin' girl."

"Love you too, Dad."

He nodded, swallowed, and grunted. Removing his hands, he dipped in, and kissed my temple while I hugged him tightly around the waist. He stepped back, cleared his throat, and reached out to punch Texas on the arm.

"She's yours to take care of, and you'd better do a fuckin' good job as her husband."

"I will, Prez."

He tipped his chin up. "I know." Dad turned and stalked out of the shop, leaving Texas and me alone.

My man pulled me around to face him, hands on my hips. "If that's him now, babe, I'm gonna hate to see what he'll be like on our weddin' day."

My bottom lip trembled, more happy tears welling. "Wedding day. We're getting married, Texas."

He threaded his fingers through my hair and tugged me closer. "Can't fuckin' wait to have you as my wife, Maya."

"I love you, baby."

"Love you too, gorgeous," he said against my lips and then gave me a slow and sweet kiss. "You reckon we got time to fuck before anyone comes lookin' for us?"

Laughing, I shook my head. "You lost your chance. Let's go party, and I promise I'll make it up to you later."

"Lookin' forward to it and our future."

Me too, and even if we spent the rest of our lives as we already were, I would be the happiest woman, already content with what we had.

Well... unless we had a child together. But that would be down the track.

UNTITLED

Read on for a look inside the Diamond MC,
with my newest MC series that starts with Country.

PROLOGUE

DUSTY

PAST

I stood in the compound with my heart in my throat as I looked around at all the men and women mingling. The women flirted so easily with the men. Envy flickered to life in my chest, wishing I had their skills. There was someone I wanted to approach, but my nerves were controlling me, and I couldn't get my feet to move from the floor, away from the wall I leaned against.

Still, my eyes stayed glued to the tall, wide man on the far side as he spoke with his biker club brothers. He wasn't the one who'd interviewed me for a position, but I wished I had met him that day. At least I would have a name to put with the handsome face. His smile was radiant, his eyes soft and ones I could get lost in. His cropped dark-brown hair, where it was a little longer at the top, called for my fingers to run through it. I would have to get on my tippy-toes to achieve it, but I'd be willing to do so.

He threw his head back and laughed. A heavy breath fell from my lips, and I quickly bit down on my bottom one when I pictured myself kissing him right there on his tattooed neck. I even wanted to know what his neatly trimmed goatee and moustache felt like against my skin.

I probably looked like a stalking weirdo leaning against the wall and watching, and that was the only reason why I pushed off the wall and walked to the bar. As soon as I reached it, I sat on one of the few empty stools and rested my elbows on the top of the counter.

A guy around my age, or maybe a bit older, stopped in front of me. "Hey, what can I get you?"

"Um, a beer, please. But I, ah, don't have an ID on me." Why did I add that? Now I'd acted underage like I was at nineteen. Not that it didn't stop me from stealing out of my parents' liquor cabinet on the nights I was bored and extra lonely.

He grinned. "No need for one here. I'll grab you a beer." When he placed the bottle in front of me, we got to talking about random things, and before I knew it, I'd had another few drinks and was feeling slightly buzzed. I swung around on the stool with a giggle as I searched for the man who'd caught my attention. Even as I talked to Kylo, who was a prospect, I couldn't stop from searching out the man. I wanted to ask Kylo who he was, but the words died in my throat each time.

Though, with my spin on the stool, I couldn't find him anywhere, and my shoulders sagged at the thought of him leaving. It wasn't until I finished turning that I noticed a form close to my side. When I lifted my gaze, my eyes nearly bugged out my head, and I almost fell backward off my stool. *He* was there. Right there. He quickly reached out and took my arm, steadying me.

Once he saw I wasn't going to crash to the floor, his hand disappeared, and he smiled down at me. It was the first time in my life my clit pulsed from a smile.

"Ah, hey, hi, hello," I blurted, blushing. I glanced to the side to see if Kylo caught my stupidity, but he was serving someone else a drink, thankfully.

"Hey, darlin'." His voice was like a warm caress that hinted towards something orgasmic. If the sound was something to roll in, I would have got naked and jumped in. I couldn't believe he was standing right in front of me, and I was gaping like a fool.

Quickly, I snapped my jaw and waved, like I hadn't just told him hello three times in one sentence. His grin widened.

"You're new, yeah?"

"Uh-huh." I couldn't look away from him or form more words in my brain.

His chuckle had me wanting to tear off my panties and throw them at him. He took a sip of his beer, and there was that neck again, on show and waiting for my lips. I gripped the stool under me to keep from jumping at him.

"Dusty," I blurted when he'd looked away. I wanted his attention back.

"That your name?"

"Yep. Do you want a beer? I mean, I can buy you one."

He smirked. "Don't need to buy drinks here, babe, but I'll have one with you."

I wanted to palm my face. I forgot we didn't pay for drinks at the compoundall the booze was supplied. At least he wasn't running from how I'd acted. "I'd like that..."

"Country."

"Country," I muttered under my breath as he called out to Kylo for two beers after glancing at my empty bottle. I peered down to his thick tattooed arms and then to his vest, my eyes widened when I saw the patch read, President.

He was in charge of the club, and all I could think was that it would have to be a hard job to do since there were so many members.

Country passed the beer to me. When I took the bottle, I tipped it his way. "Thanks. Can I ask you something?"

He nodded. "Yeah, Dusty." Oh boy, my name from his mouth sounded like porn.

"I... can't remember now."

He chuckled. "Then let me ask you somethin'."

Smiling, I nodded. I took a sip of the beer, kicking my feet since they didn't touch the ground.

His gaze made a quick run over me, and instead of feeling creeped out, I liked it. "How old are you?"

With a mock glare, I gasped. "You should never start with the age question."

His dark brow rose, and a chuckle sounded, this one softer. "I shouldn't?"

"No. Not unless you're prepared to answer it as well."

"All right, darlin'. You go first."

"Nineteen."

His eyes widened. "No shit?"

Shaking my head, I replied with his own words, "No shit."

"Babe" was all he said with a shake of his head.

"What?"

He rested his elbows on the counter and turned his head my way. "What you doin' here?"

Picking up my drink, I shook it a little. "Drinking."

"Nah, darlin', I mean what are you doin' at a clubhouse at nineteen? Don't you got better things to do? Go out with friends, people your own age?"

"No, I don't have many friends who I feel comfortable drinking with." Coffee dates, sure, but nothing where I felt I could let myself go and drink around them. I'd be too worried about what I'd say or do or if they found me annoying.

Yet, there I was drinking in a biker's club of all places.

Yeah, my actions didn't make sense.

My face heated. "I know it doesn't make sense because here I am drinking with you, but..."

"But?"

Shrugging, I took a sip of the beer and looked up at him. "I guess I feel safe here." Strange, even to my own mind. But I couldn't understand why, when I walked in there, I felt a sense of home.

He jerked his head back as if surprised by my answer.

"And don't think I didn't realize you didn't answer me about your age."

"I'm thirty-eight, babe." I didn't like the way his brows pinched together or the fact he looked away. I was sure my being younger was a problem for him.

"Um, I just wanted you to know that I don't think you're old."

He threw his head back and laughed. "Good to know, darlin'. What made you join as a club girl, Dusty?"

"I overheard some women talking at a coffee shop about it." I pointed behind him. "Those two over there." He didn't look away from me. "I thought it was time to do something different in my life, and that decision took me here."

"No shit?"

Laughing, I shrugged. "No shit." It also happened to be at a time I was low and bored with my life.

He took one elbow off the bar and turned his body my way. My pulse raced when he reached out and tucked my light brown hair behind my ear. He caught the shiver it caused.

"You seriously don't care I'm way older?" He cocked a brow.

"No. Not at all."

"Good to know. Tell me somethin' about you, Dusty."

So I did, and we ended up talking for an hour, which included some light touches, knee bumps when he sat on his own stool, and many flirty smiles. It was the best fun I'd had in a long time, and I was glad I had those drinks to push my nerves back, as it meant I got to know Country and talk somewhat normally.

The crowded room had lessened a bit by the time Country stood from his stool. He gently pinched my chin to tilt my head back to have my gaze. My stomach put on a display of flips and twists. Was this where he was going to leave? I didn't want to see him go. I was enjoying my time with him. He'd made me laugh more tonight than I had in a long time.

"What do you want, Dusty?"

"P-Pardon?"

His eyes warmed. "Tell me what you want, darlin'."

"As in with my future or... tonight?"

He smiled. "Tonight, baby."

Baby. He said it in a way that had me feeling all soft inside.

With both hands, I reached up and gripped his inked wrist. I was going to take a leap. Take something I wanted from the moment I first saw him. "I..." I blew out a breath. "I'd like to go to bed with you."

His gaze darkened as he leaned in and kissed the corner of my mouth. His facial hair was rough, but I liked the way it tickled against my skin. "Then let's go to bed, darlin'." He took hold of my hand and led me through the compound and up some stairs to a room at the back. His room.

My hands shook from a jumble of nerves and excitement. When I heard his bedroom door close, I jolted and turned to him.

His brows rose as he watched my chest rise and fall rapidly. "You sure you want this, darlin'? You can walk out that door any time you want."

"No, I mean, yes, please." My face burned. "What I'm trying to say is that... well, I couldn't walk out that door because I like where I am." *I want this. Please take me now.* His smile at my ramblings was a little smug, but I didn't mind. Even though it seemed my nerves were coming back.

"Fuck, darlin', you're somethin' special. I'm sure that's why the brothers didn't snap you up."

Or it could have been because they saw how I couldn't keep my gaze away from Country. Thankfully, the man himself didn't seem to notice my attention on him most of the night... before he approached.

Butterflies took flight inside me from knowing how lucky I was Country had come to the bar and stood beside me. If he hadn't, I would have gone back to my room dejected. When I'd first applied to be a club girl, Death, the man who'd interviewed me, made it clear the brothers would never force themselves on the girls. We had to be willing and wanting their attention.

Boy, did I want Country's.

He took a few steps to stop in front of me. My skin buzzed when he cupped my cheeks with both tattooed hands and slowly bent. His lips headed right towards mine, and I watched his eyes flick over my face, as if he was waiting for me to freak and stop this.

That wasn't going to happen.

His lips pressed against mine in a quick taste before he pulled back and caught my gaze. His touch wasn't enough. I *needed* more.

Lifting my hands, I slid them up under his vest and gripped his tee before stretching up for a better taste. When I tugged him closer and nipped at his plump bottom lip, he groaned and moved one hand to the back of my head. The kiss deepened. We opened to each other, exploring one another's mouth in a heated, hot kiss that had my toes curling.

Feeling brave, I dropped a hand to his perfect ass and took a handful that brought him in closer, where I felt his erection against my stomach. I wanted him in my mouth. Just thinking that had my body shivering and a moan slipping out. Country broke the kiss to clip, "Christ, darlin'." His heated gaze fell to my mouth, and he muttered, "Your mouth... fuck."

"C-Can I... I want to....'

His fingers threaded through the back of my hair and gripped, tearing a gasp out of me.

"Fuckin' beautiful. What you want, darlin'?"

"To suck you."

He groaned and rested his forehead against mine for a moment before his lips brushed against my cheek, my nose, the corner of my mouth. There he ordered gruffly, "Go sit on the edge of the bed." As soon as his hands fell away, I scrambled over to the bed and sat, looking up at him with my hands on my lap.

"Fuck me," he muttered with a smirk. I watched as he moved around the room, took off his vest, hung it on the back of a chair, and then removed his tee. His smooth, strong chest had my mouth watering. Across his chest was a tattoo, surrounded by others, of written words of the club's name. I wanted to reach out and trace them with my finger.

Later though, because as he started my way, he popped the button on his jeans. I rubbed my thighs together as my pussy pulsed. He slid the zipper down as he stopped in front of me. "Last chance, sugar. If you're havin' second thoughts, walk out. If you're not and want my cock in your mouth, then know this will be your only chance to go. As soon as this starts, I'm not gonna be able to stop."

"Country, I'm not going anywhere."

A growl rumbled out of him that had me running my hands up the back of his thighs to grip the top of his jeans and slowly pull them down. His cock popped free. The tip glistened with precum. He took himself in hand and held it out for me. When I went to dip in, he shook his head.

"Close your mouth, darlin'." I did, and my heart stumbled when he squeezed the base of his cock and brought his hand up his length, causing the tip to leak even more. He cupped the back of my head and rested his wet tip against my lips, running it over and around my lips.

He groaned, his chest rising and falling faster. "Fuckin' gorgeous. Open up now, baby."

I did and licked at the tip before flicking my tongue around the head. Country made a noise in the back of his throat and jutted his hips forward, sliding his cock deeper into my mouth.

"Jesus, Dusty. I can't...." Wait, what? Panic started to ebb its way in, until he shifted back enough to bend, take hold of my tee, and pull it over my head. His hands were on my bra next, and his fingers were quick to undo it and fling it from my body. Next, he shoved my shoulder where I dropped back on the bed with a gasp, but I didn't mind at all, not when Country tugged my jeans and panties from me and threw them over his head as his gaze ran over my body.

Smiling, I now understood what he'd meant by he couldn't. He didn't want to wait. Already he was at the point of needing to be inside me, and I was more than willing to give him that.

"You've got me feelin' like a schoolboy, Dusty," he clipped through clenched teeth.

A laugh escaped. I covered my mouth, but he'd already heard it.

His brow rose. "You think it's funny?"

Pinching my thumb and finger together, I said, "A little."

Another growl sounded in the room as he grabbed my ankle and dragged me to the edge of the bed causing me to squeal. He bit inside my thigh, ripping a moan from my mouth.

"I'll have to punish you for laughin', darlin'."

Panting, I shook my head and looked down at him trailing kisses and nips inside of each thigh. "Can... can you do that later, please?"

He lifted his head. "Why, baby?"

Cupping my breast, I swallowed and told him the truth. "Because I need you inside me."

"Fuck. Fuck." He reached into his jeans pocket, grabbed his wallet, and pulled out a condom. I watched him rip it open and slide it on, and in the next second, he hooked my legs around his waist and pushed inside me. Arching, I cried out and wrapped my arms around his neck, needing him as close as possible.

"Baby, Christ, you fit me like a glove." He kissed my neck and slowly pulled out, only to return with a grunt. "Perfect. So fuckin' perfect."

"Country," I whispered before I sank my teeth into his shoulder. He groaned into my ear. His hips pulled back to slam into me, and I moaned around his skin, then licked the spot. "Yes, honey."

"Fuck, fuck, fuck," he muttered, sliding his hands down under my ass where he gripped, the speed of his thrusts increasing. I dropped my head back, panting and loving the way he filled me up, pressing me in all the right areas.

"God, yes." I glided a hand from his shoulder up and tugged on his hair. He gave me what I wanted by lifting his mouth from sucking on my neck to my lips. The kiss was long, slow, and amazing with the hard thrusts of his cock. My lower belly tingled. My pussy tightened around him, drawing out a grunted growl from him into my mouth. I drank it down and held him tighter. I moved my lips from him, panting out, "Close, honey."

He groaned, taking my lips in a wild kiss. I dropped my head to the bed and moaned, clamping around his cock as I came.

"Jesus, baby. You love my cock."

"Oh, yeah."

He cursed under his breath, then licked along my neck, biting my lobe where I heard the hitch in his breath and groan as he fucked me faster, filling the condom. He slowed his thrust, leisurely moving in and out of me until he stopped and looked down at me.

His gaze ran over my face, my breasts, and back up. When he had my eyes again, he grinned, and I couldn't stop the returning smile.

"Enjoyed that, darlin'."

"Me too."

"Good." He pulled out of me, and I *felt* the loss right away. Sitting up when he shifted away, I curled my arms around my knees and watched him get rid of the condom before doing up his jeans again. I wanted him again, but I could already see he was shutting that idea down when he pulled a new tee over his body.

It was then I knew my place. I was only a club girl, after all.

Quickly, I slipped off the bed and got dressed, ignoring the way disappointment twisted my stomach. I'd asked for this by joining as a club girl. It couldn't be any different between us, and really, I shouldn't have wanted it to after one night together.

I didn't know what the future had in store, but I would make it one where I was happy. Where I was welcome and not a nuisance.

Moving to the door, I glanced over my shoulder to see Country looking at his phone in hand with a pinched brow.

"Um, later."

He looked up, smiled, and lifted his chin my way. That was his goodbye. I took it because I wasn't there for something more. Well, that was what I would keep reminding myself.

CHAPTER ONE

DUSTY

PRESENT

*F*rom the corner of the room, I watched as
Country flirted with his new woman of the
week, Rochelle. To me, it sounded like she was related to a
roach. I hated her even before I met her. Pathetic, right? It
wasn't like I was in love with Country. We'd slept together
a couple of times, one before and then after his breakup
with a different girl. Isla. Both of us had been a little tipsy
each time.

So why can't you get him off your mind?
Shut up, stupid brain.

I didn't know why my eyes sought him out whenever I

entered the compound. Or why my belly clenched when I caught other club ladies flirting with him, or why my heart turned into a wildly buzzing vibrator whenever he smiled or winked at me.

All right, I did know, but I wasn't going to let my little crush stick.

Not when I could save myself from hurt, since I knew, and I *definitely* knew, he was a player. He liked younger women, which I was, right along with a heap of other club girls.

I could have pussy punched myself for joining as a club girl when I didn't even need to. I didn't have bad parents. I didn't have someone to hide from or someone after me, as far as I knew. So why did I join? Because I wanted something different and exciting in my life, and when I'd first applied to become one of the club women in the Diamond MC¾where I wouldn't sleep with anyone outside of the club¾they promised I wouldn't have to have sex with every member. *I* could pick. That was two years ago, when I was a lot more nervous and shy, and the only member I had slept with was Country.

Why did I only pick him? Why did I feel that sleeping with someone else would be the wrong move? Especially when Country didn't care. He'd been with a few others.

Shaking my head, I took a sip of my vodka and cranberry and turned away from Country. I loved being in the compound. The atmosphere made me feel lighter on the inside. There were always people around to talk to, so I never felt lonely like when I went home to my parents' house.

Lonely had been my middle name for as long as I could remember. My parents loved me and always treated me well enough, but they were busy people. They explained they needed to work long hours because they wanted a future where they could retire without having financial worries. I understood. I did.

Rolling my eyes, I pushed them from my mind; it wasn't the time to think about how lonely I'd allowed myself to get. I had friends, but I didn't have anyone I ran to with my problems. It was my own fault for not opening up to people. The last thing I wanted was to be a bother.

Taking another sip of my drink, I looked to the bar and smiled. Kylo, or as his brothers called him, Gun, was leaning against the bar and walking two fingers up his husband's chest, Saint, with a flirty smile. I'd been surprised, like a lot of us in the club, when they'd gotten together, but anyone now could see the love they had for each other. My gaze snagged on another married couple. Wreck, who had always come across as a beefy asshole, was staring down at his husband, Lucas, while Lucas talked to State and Courtney, waving his hand wildly as he spoke. Wreck had shocked everyone more than Gun and Saint had. A few members weren't happy to have gay men in the club, but Country had put a stop to the complaints and said if anyone did have an issue, they could leave.

That was another reason why I'd stayed with the Diamond MC. I liked how Country ran things. He was fair but also stood up for things he strongly believed in¾one was supporting his brothers and who they loved, no matter the gender.

"You seem to be thinkin' a lot tonight." Tech stepped up beside me with a smile. He took a drag from his beer, and I watched his throat move over the motion. Could I imagine sleeping with Tech? He was very good-looking.

Realizing he was waiting for an answer, I blushed and nodded. "Yeah, my mind's not my friend tonight." There were only a few members I felt comfortable and could be myself with. Tech was one of them, along with Country, though he did fluster me since I'd seen him naked. There were also Gun and Quake.

"Need a hand to get your mind off things?" Tech's smile grew flirty as he leaned his arm against the wall, facing me. Another great thing about the club was that when a woman said no, the men listened. Well, most did. There were only a few who tried to be persistent, but when their brothers yelled to knock it off, they did. They respected women, and I honestly felt safe in the compound.

The question I was fluffing around with was wondering if I could get my mind off Country by sleeping with Tech. With a quick glance across the room, where I saw Country kissing the roach on the cheek, I sipped my drink as my stomach clenched and looked up at Tech.

I cocked a brow. "What did you have in mind?"

His gaze ran over me slowly. "I could think of a few things."

He'd always been the biggest flirt with me, and I did enjoy his attention. I locked my eyes on his lips. Yeah, I could imagine kissing them.

"Would these things happen to be in private?"

"Definitely."

A shiver swept over me when he glided a couple of fingers over my cheek, and he gently brushed his thumb against my bottom lip.

Before his hand dropped, I sneaked my tongue out and licked over his thumb. His eyes darkened as he straightened.

"Dusty." My name was clipped off with desire.

"Just to confirm, nothing will change between us?" That was what I wanted most, because until I got over my... whatever it was with Country, I wanted to make sure Tech and I would stay friends.

"Baby, I ain't lookin' for anythin' long-term. Are you cool with that?"

"Cool as a cucumber." Okay, that sounded cheesy, but it had Tech chuckling, at least.

He nodded toward the hall where the bedrooms lay. "You wanna take a walk with me?"

I did. Didn't I?

I did because I loved sex, and I could use a little loving. Maybe even more experience would be good than having only two lovers. One had been my high school sweetheart, the other Country, and Lord knew I needed to move on from him, especially since he hadn't been looking for anything serious those two times I'd slept with him. I worked that out quickly when I'd woken in the morning and he'd pretty much said, "Thanks for a good night, Dust," and that was it.

Cocking my head to the side, I replied, "Depends." Reaching out my hand, I waited for him to take it.

When he did, Tech smirked and ran his thumb over the back of my hand. "On what?"

A shadow covered half of Tech's face, and we both looked to see Country standing there.

"Prez, what's up?"

Country crossed his arms over his wide chest. A chest I had seen naked. A chest I knew looked amazing. Still, Tech's could be just as good, and I had to give him a chance since the other man in front of me wasn't interested. Over his shoulder, I saw the roach stalking over. My upper lip rose, but I quickly took a sip of my drink.

"Need you to do somethin' for me."

Tech's eyes widened a little as he dropped my hand. "Now?"

"Babe, I slip off to the restroom for a second and you're gone. What are you doing over here?" the roach asked as she wound her arms around his waist.

Jealousy uncurled inside me and bared its fangs. I stomped on the emotion, having no right to be anything with Country.

"Just dealin' with business, Chelle. Go grab us a drink, yeah?"

After she planted a claiming kiss to his cheek and

glared at me, which was unnecessary, she swayed her hips over to the bar.

Straightening, I smiled at Tech when he looked my way. "I'll leave you both to it. When you're not busy, come find me." I poked him in the side and walked away. If I looked at Country, I worried he and Tech would see something I didn't want to show.

At the bar, as far away from the roach as possible, I placed my empty glass down and waited for the new prospect's attention.

"Dusty, settle something for me." Gun and Saint stepped up beside me. Over their shoulders, I caught another glare from the roach. What was her problem? I hadn't flirted with Country in front of her, and I tried to keep my gazes non-stalkerish. Did he tell her we'd slept together? If he did, he must have mentioned how long ago the last time was.

Six months, two days, and fourteen hours.

That's what I got for having a good memory.

Ignoring her, I smiled at the two men in front of me. "What do you need settled?"

"Prospect," Saint suddenly called. "Get Dusty the usual, yeah?"

"On it."

Gun clapped, and my gaze switched back to him after a grateful smile to Saint. "Right, tell Saint that you think it's better to give head than receive it."

It was lucky I wasn't drinking anything. I still gaped like a fish, not expecting that type of question.

"Wouldn't it be better to ask Wreck and Lucas or West and Adrik, since you all have to"—I leaned in to whisper —"suck dick, and it's different for me because I have a vagina, and I don't have a partner?"

Gun shook his head. "Doesn't matter about you having a pussy—"

"Poor girl," Saint muttered.

Gun and I stared at him. "You think I'm a poor girl for having a vagina?"

"Babe" was all he said, an amused glint in his eyes.

"I think I'm offended on her behalf." Gun smacked Saint in the stomach. "She's fine the way she is, even with her having a pussy."

We were starting to gain some looks, since Gun spoke loudly. My face burned, and I quickly took a gulp of my drink that the prospect placed on the bar.

"Can we stop talking about my vagina?" I urged frantically.

Gun winked. "Will do, as long as you answer the question. Do you prefer to give or receive?"

"You seriously want me to answer it?"

"Yes."

"But why?" It may have sounded a little whiny.

"Saint's a greedy bastard who likes to receive over give, but I'll forgive the douche if we get more people to agree with his side."

"And if I don't, then you'll be shitty at Saint for a while?"

Gun nodded. "Yes."

Grinning evilly, I clicked my fingers and pointed at Gun. "I'd rather give."

Saint snorted. "She's only sayin' it because she wants you pissed at me for sayin' what I did about her and her pussy."

"Oh my God, stop talking about my pu—vagina," I bit out in a low tone. "But seriously, I'm telling the truth." I did prefer to give a nice head job than receive one in return, as I always got shy when a guy was between my legs. I didn't understand why men enjoyed doing that to women when it was like an open wound down there.

Country sure liked it.

I didn't need that reminder.

I set my drink back on the bar and ran a hand through my light brown hair while Saint and Gun argued some more. Picking at a couple of strands, I pulled it up to look at it. My hair wasn't anything special, a boring color, really. I glanced over at the roach, who had her arm curled around Country's waist while he spoke with another member. I hated to admit it, but she had amazing long blonde hair that seemed full of life and not dull like mine.

Oh hell no. I wasn't comparing myself to her.

No way.

"Dusty, hey." Courtney stepped up with a smile and her one-year-old on her hip.

"Hi, Court. How are things?" She was State's woman, and they were set to get married in a couple of months. To me, they were the perfect couple. Courtney had been a godsend with the club girls. Since she became an old lady, the bitchiness was cut down, a schedule was made for cleaning and cooking, and she was so nice it hurt my teeth sometimes.

"Court, I have a question for you," Gun said.

"Abort. Run, Court, run." I gently shoved at her side, but she only laughed.

"What question?"

"Do you prefer to give or receive head?"

"Receive," she said instantly. "State does this thing with his tongue that—"

Saint covered her mouth. "Dear God, woman, we don't need to hear anythin' about State and his tongue. Especially not in front of young ears." He dropped his hand and turned to Gun. "Still, I appreciate your honesty." Saint crossed his arms over his chest and smirked at his husband.

Gun shot him the middle finger. "I'm gonna ask some more first." He quickly walked off and called out to Country. I didn't want to hear Country's answer, so I excused myself. When I didn't see Tech anywhere, I went up to the rooms supplied to the club girls and entered my own. I didn't have the energy to drive home to an empty house, knowing my parents would be either away on a trip for work or in their offices. I liked staying at the compound because there was always noise in the background.

I hoped Tech would finish whatever Country had him doing soon, and when he did, he'd come to my room. I had to move on. I had to let go of this infatuation and how it had controlled me for far too long.

The first step to get over him would be to sleep with another brother. If that didn't work, maybe, just maybe, it was time for me to move on from the compound. I worried I was sticking around here for all the wrong reasons. Like this place was the only way to fix my loneliness. Could it be possible I was going about things the wrong way? Was I supposed to be out in the world finding friends and dating someone who had nothing to do with the club?

Maybe.

ACKNOWLEDGMENTS

It was great stepping back into the Hawks MC. I hope you've enjoyed it as much as I have writing about Texas and Maya. I wanted to thank you for sticking with me and this series and want to explain why there's a wait between each book. If I write them too close together, I get bored and don't enjoy writing the story. Sometimes, I need the break between books to refresh my mind so I can try to make the Hawks MC fresh and still loveable for everyone.

I also wanted to thank the bloggers and promotional companies for sharing and helping spread the word about Texas. Authors would be lost without you all.

As always, a big thanks goes to Becky, and her team, at Hot Tree Editing. All of you are a pleasure to work with. x

To Lindsey Lawson, you've stuck with me from the start, and I'll always appreciate your help and support.

To my beta readers, you know who you are, thank you for getting back into the Hawks with me and for your assistance.

ALSO BY LILA ROSE

Hawks MC: Ballarat Charter

Holding Out (Free)

Outplayed (standalone related to the Hawks MC)

Climbing Out

Finding Out (novella)

Black Out

No Way Out

Coming Out (m/m novella)

Out to Find Freedom (standalone related to the Hawks MC)

Hawks MC: Caroline Springs Charter

The Secret's Out

Hiding Out

Down and Out

Living Without

Walkout (novella)

Hear Me Out (m/m)

Break Out (novella)

Fallout

Out of the Blue (standalone related to the Hawks MC: m/m/m)

Out Gamed (standalone related to the Hawks MC: novella)

Hawks MC: next generation

Coyote

Ruin (m/m)

Texas

Swan

Romania

Polished P & P series (m/m romance)

Wreck Me Forever

Never a Saint

Working Out West

Up in a Blaze

Diamond MC

Country

State

Death

Torch

Romantic Comedies

Making Changes

Making Sense

***

Fumbled Love

Bumbled Love